Skies of Fire

Lenore Edwards

StoneFire Press

ISBN: 978-0-9835537-4-8 print
ISBN: 978-0-9835537-0-0 eBook

Published by StoneFire Press,
a division of Adria Firestone International, LLC.
www.lenoreedwards.com

Chapter One

Karl Van Ness dropped his glass. The heavy crystal tumbler shattered on the marble floor. Some of the guests milling in the grand ballroom turned to stare as he casually flicked the splashes of scotch from his perfectly tailored double-breasted dinner jacket. No one saw his hands shaking.

Handsome and outwardly calm, he made it seem the most natural gesture in the world, his strong elegant hands brushing the spots from the grosgrain lapels with his silk handkerchief. Smiling, the onlookers soon turned back to their own conversations as a waiter began collecting the shards of glass, white-gloved hands carefully placing the fragments on a silver tray.

"May I bring you another drink, Sir?" inquired the maître'd.

"I'll take another Dalwhinne on the rocks, thanks, Tom." Karl spoke evenly, struggling to conceal the shock he was feeling. He was not a man easily flustered. Despite the ease of his attitude there was no mistaking the natural aura of power and authority he commanded over others, and at this moment, over himself.

"What on earth is the matter, Karl?" resonated a beautifully modulated voice. Slowly, deliberately, he turned to meet the dark eyes and concerned gaze of his friend, Evelyn.

Evelyn St. John, draped in a floor-length, black silk crepe gown, was a picture of classic beauty. A pearl satin drape accentuated the open back that exposed her flawless skin. The matching satin French cuffs ornamented with diamond cufflinks added the perfect touch of elegance.

At forty-nine Evelyn was a stunningly attractive woman, with peaked eyebrows, shoulder-length mahogany hair, an aquiline nose, fine cheekbones, and a generous mouth. She looked better than most women of twenty-nine. Her dark eyes, unable to conceal the wisdom of life experience, were the only hint of her true age.

Noticing the muscles tighten in his jaw and the almost imperceptible flair to his nostrils, she gently placed a slender, manicured hand on his left arm. The lustrous solitaire she wore glimmered against the texture of his jacket.

"Karl?" she spoke quietly, worry creasing her brow. She didn't need to be touching him to feel the tension in his body. He wasn't looking at Evelyn, but staring right through her, lost in a disturbing trance.

"Karl? Karl, snap out of it! Look at me. What is it?" demanded Evelyn.

He looked at her for a moment, eyes full of unspeakable memories. She saw the familiar shadow of pain veil his face. Following his stare as he turned toward the main entrance of the ballroom, she caught sight of the stunning woman who had just entered.

Involuntarily, Evelyn caught her breath. Her hand still resting on his arm, they stood silently, incapable of speech, staring at the striking beauty who was turning all heads. It was Evelyn who finally broke the silence.

"It's your ghost, isn't it?"

Karl stood rigid, his face an implacable granite mask, eyes fixed with a steely glint upon the figure in the doorway. Face void of expression, in a strangled voice he whispered, "Yes . . . it's her."

If Ashton Cameron had any doubts about what to wear, they vanished the moment she swept into the grand ballroom of the new Osprey Hotel. Shimmering in a champagne-colored dress of bugle beads that caressed the curves of her voluptuous figure, she was a combination of the exotic and the seductive. All eyes turned to gaze at her as she confidently made her entrance.

An almost indecently high split in her gown revealed the silken flesh of her left thigh as her high-heeled satin sandals tapped her unique tattoo on the marble floor. She smiled to herself at her choice of attire, the plunging sweetheart neckline enhanced her exquisite torso and shoulders. Both classic and sexy, it was as if the gown had been sewn onto her body.

It had been a long flight from New York City to Sydney and she was glad for the rest she had taken in the afternoon, and the relief of a much-needed warm soak in the tub. Despite the comfort of first class travel, she hadn't slept much — there had been too much on her mind, as usual. Still, she had managed to use the travel time wisely, reviewing all the material she had on the man being touted as the most talented architect of the decade.

She wanted this interview in earnest, and worked hard to convince her father that she was the best qualified journalist at Cameron House for the task. Her father had finally given in after much deliberation. "Well, if anyone is going to get the scoop on this ladykiller, it's you. You are, after all, one of the company's best assets, and my greatest achievement." Ashton recalled the warmth and pride in his smile.

"Daddy, put your mind at rest. I'm old enough to take care of myself, and I'll have you know I'm impervious to his kind!"

She chuckled to herself remembering how her father just shook his head and sighed.

Ashton's gray-green eyes scanned the ballroom. She made a mental note of the highly polished marble floors, the rich mahogany bar skirted by marble, the warmth of the rosewood paneling. The glittering chandeliers and the full length French doors opened onto a spectacular view of Sydney Harbour.

"Very impressive!" she thought. It was as plush and opulent as the press releases had described. She quickly assessed there were at least 500 guests milling about enjoying the hospitality. It certainly was a gala event, a befitting grand opening for this new luxury hotel.

Who was he among this crowd, she wondered? Looking about her, she did a double take of a very handsome, dark haired man standing by the bar. Wiping his jacket, he'd apparently had a minor mishap with his drink. I'll bet that doesn't happen to him very often, she mused, appreciating his commanding presence.

Even from across a crowded room, it was impossible to conceal the strength and poise of his hard body beneath the beautiful lines of his tuxedo.

Ashton was surprised to find herself thinking that he was the most interesting man in the room. It was with some mirth that she realized she even felt a small pang of jealousy toward the elegant woman by his side. Her stomach told her he was not a man to be toyed with, and she tried vainly to remind herself that she had enough on her plate already.

With difficulty, she turned back to her task at hand. Did gifted architects have a particular look, she wondered. How ridiculous not to have a picture to go by.

She hadn't believed it at first, when she had been told that there was no photographic record of him; it seemed too ridiculous in this age of information technology. How could a man with such a reputation, both as an architect and a ladykiller, not have been photographed somewhere? She didn't like being at a disadvantage.

Still, there was something fascinating about a man who wanted his buildings, rather than his good looks, to speak for him. His philosophy and view of the world would make for a fascinating interview. Fascinating . . . if it were true.

Chapter Two

"May I offer you a drink?"

Ashton turned to find a pair of intense blue eyes boring into her. Silently catching her breath, she momentarily forgot where she was, trapped by the mesmerizing stare. She knew those eyes, but it couldn't be — he was dead. Why was her heart racing? No, pull yourself together, girl! This man is shorter, his voice is different, the hardness of his body, the breadth of his shoulders too wide.

"May I offer you a drink?" Asked the same deep, husky voice. Ashton felt herself shudder involuntarily. Up close the man she had been watching was even more disturbing. God, she thought, his voice is so full of . . . of promises. She didn't know how else to define it.

"Oh, thank you, but not tonight." Ashton managed to find her voice. She wondered if she really sounded as unnerved as she felt. Why was this man making her so nervous? She almost couldn't believe he was standing beside her, smiling, charming, offering her a glass of champagne. He was so close the scent of him assailed her senses.

"But surely, Miss. . . ."

"Miss Cameron," she offered.

"But surely Miss Cameron, you could make an exception. This is no ordinary champagne you know, it's Veuve Clicquot Rosé. And this is a very special occasion after all."

Ashton wondered why he uttered his last sentence that way. She stood looking into those impenetrable blue eyes. She never thought she would see eyes that blue again — the deep unfathomable blue of the ocean. No, she didn't have time for those memories . . . not here, not now. She needed all her wits about her.

"Is there something the matter, Miss Cameron?"

"Ashton, please call me Ashton. And no, there is nothing the matter." He held out the fluted glass to her.

"Well, if you insist . . ."

"I do."

His fingers briefly brushed hers, purposely she realized later, as he handed the glass to her. It was the touch of high voltage wires.

Steadying her voice, attempting to smile unconcernedly, she asked, "Aren't you going to join me?"

"I only drink Dalwhinne," he smiled, deliberately caressing a crystal tumbler in his left hand. She felt the urge to blush, watching the way he held the glass. She was annoyed at herself for not having noticed it before. A fine journalist she was, she mused, too busy gazing into his eyes like some stunned rabbit.

"To true love," he said, raising his glass to hers. "You believe in that, don't you?"

As she raised the champagne to her lips, Ashton had the distinct impression that she was in trouble. "Is this your first visit to Australia . . . Ashton?" He paused, savoring the sound of her name.

"Yes, I've never been here before."

"When did you arrive?"

"Just this morning."

"Did you have a pleasant flight?"

"Yes, thank you. I suppose you're going to ask me about the in-flight service as well," she quipped.

His third degree was beginning to rile her, prompting a very deliberate casualness.

Undeterred he continued, "So, what brings you to this part of this world?"

"Oh, I've heard so much about the wonders of the Great Barrier Reef. It's the perfect chance to enjoy some sun and surf, and . . ."

"Really? You don't appear to be in need of a tan."

Ashton was more than aware of the smoldering blue eyes lazily following the curves of her body. His gaze worked its way up her length, pausing to savor for a moment her revealed thigh, almost scalding her with its intensity, before continuing his appraisal. Upwards, over the flatness of her taut stomach, taking in the outline of her firm, round breasts, traveling the length of her slender neck, before meeting the indignant flash of the gray-green eyes. He was enjoying himself all too much, she fumed.

"I'm not here just for pleasure, you know!" she snapped.

He merely raised an eyebrow quizzically, his face the picture of innocence. She understood his insinuation, there was no need for words. He really was a most disconcerting man, possessing a kind of arrogant charm that made him almost irresistible; but she was not about to play his game.

"I think you're a little lost. Sydney is a long way from the Barrier Reef." His voice was full of mocking laughter.

"I'm here to interview Karl Van Ness," she stated with authority, secretly hoping to impress him with her revelation.

"Are you?" There was a slight upturning at the corners of his mouth. A very gentle mouth, Ashton noted, unusual for a man with such a hard face and strong jaw.

"Do you know him?"

"We are acquainted."

"Is he here tonight?"

"I would think so. This is his building after all."

"What is he like?"

"Different things to different people, I suspect."

It suddenly occurred to Ashton that she was engaged in conversation with a complete stranger. "I don't believe I caught your name," she ventured.

A muscle twitched in his jaw. "I don't believe I dropped it."

The unmitigated nerve of this man. No matter how attractive he might be Ashton had no intention of wasting another minute in his infuriating presence.

Karl was still in shock. She really doesn't know who I am, he thought, his head spinning. She really has no idea. Can I have changed so much? Do I really look so different? His heart was pounding. It was taking all of his self-mastery not to reveal his raging emotions. Should I tell her? Karl was jolted from his reverie by the orchestra beginning the strains of *I've Got You Under My Skin*.

Voice as smooth as silk he murmured, "Ashton, would you be in the mood. . . ."

"For what?" she demanded, preparing to leave, handing her glass to a passing waiter.

"To dance, of course." He smiled devilishly, gesturing toward the dance floor.

"I don't dance with someone I don't know."

"You do now." And with that he slipped a firm hand in the small of her back, pulled her towards him and guided her towards the dance floor.

Ashton was in no position to resist. She knew her delicate, high heeled sandals would not provide her with a sure footing on a marble floor to counter the strength of him, and the last thing she wanted right now was a scene.

Ashton was keenly aware of his strong hand possessing her waist. As he drew her closer to him, she felt a rush of adrenaline as the tips of her breasts pressed against the hardness of his chest. She was aware of the warmth of him, the length of his tall, muscular frame guiding her movements, and his scent filling her nostrils.

They moved as if they had always danced together. Feet barely touching the ground, they glided effortlessly as one. They danced without speaking, in a world all their own, guided only by the insistent rhythm of the music.

At 5'7" plus high heels, Ashton cut a regal figure, intimidating most men. However, it was clear that this handsome stranger was not most men, not in any respect.

The flesh of his smooth shaven jaw rested gently against her temple, and her head reeled as his breath gently caressed her ear. He was guiding her expertly, a combination of grace, style, and an unmistakable masculine sensuality. He was a complete enigma to her.

It was he who finally broke the spell, his tone soft, warm, and full of admiration. "Where did you learn to dance like this?"

The countless dance lessons she had taken at the Swiss finishing school at her father's insistence had certainly paid off, thought Ashton.

"A girl learns all sorts of things in many years of travel."

"Really? So you've traveled a lot?"

"Too much." Visions flashed through her mind in rapid succession — so many airports, so many different places, different foods, and different smells. After all this time, after all this activity, it was still impossible to forget. . . .

She was aware of the intense blue eyes fixed on her as if trying to read her mind.

"Though this is my first time at the bottom of the world!" she added lightly, eager to avoid too much probing. She didn't feel like discussing her life right now.

"Or the top, depending on your point of view." He smiled.

"Would you mind terribly if we got some air?" she asked.

"Are you feeling all right?"

"I'll be fine, I just need some fresh air. It's been a very long day."

"Certainly."

His hand firmly on her elbow, he steered her through the throng of couples on the dance floor to the full-length French doors that opened out onto a breathtaking view of Sydney Harbour. Ashton gasped with delight as she caught sight of the illumined sails of the Sydney Opera House against the arching curve of the Harbour Bridge.

The sky was ablaze with the last rays of the setting sun, a palette of deep red, orange, and purple hues. The colors reflected off the calm waters, bordered by a sea of thousands of tiny lights spread over the vast shoreline. The landing over Sydney Heads had afforded her a wonderful view, but the city was even more spectacular by night.

"Oh, it is so beautiful, better than I ever imagined," she whispered.

"Yes, this is one of my favorite cities." He gestured toward the unique profile of the Opera House. "Mr. Utzon was quite an architect, don't you think?

Ashton merely nodded her assent, utterly enchanted by this strange land with a fiery sky — no wonder it was known as the Land of Fire. A gentle breeze caressed her skin as she brushed aside a loose tendril of her light auburn hair. With strands of red and strawberry blonde throughout, it wasn't dissimilar to the gorgeous sunset.

Sensing that destiny had an unusual plan in store for her, she was unable to fathom the curious sensation that danced in her stomach. Why had fate brought her to the antipodes, she wondered. And who was this stranger?

Turning to get a better view of his face she found him lost in his own reverie, filled with what seemed a deep sadness. With her eyes tracing the outline of his noble face, Ashton noted appreciatively the bronze of his skin, the strong nose, the dark brows, the scar along his hairline . . .

The scar along his hairline? Ashton looked twice. Yes, that's exactly what it was, the faintest hint of a scar. Whatever had happened, the surgeon's hand had obviously been expert. A wave of tenderness engulfed her, and she would never know what prompted her next action. Almost involuntarily, guided by a force greater than herself, she reached up and lightly ran her fingers over the traces of the scar, her fingers brushing the line of his thick dark hair.

Jolting sharply at her touch, his body transformed in an instant from its easy posture to that of high-tension wires. Grasping the brass handrail in front of him, his knuckles turned white under the pressure of his grip. Perplexed, Ashton watched his face intently, trying to fathom why her touch had disturbed him so. Jaw set like concrete, eyes that but moments ago had been so full of awe for the majesty of the scene before them, were closed now, apparently focused on an unknown phantom.

For the thousandth time, Karl relived that moment ten years ago when the doctors removed his bandages. True, they had warned him that his appearance would be considerably altered but nothing could have prepared him for the shock of what greeted him. The surgeons, the best that money could buy, had rebuilt his entire face so that even he didn't recognize himself.

The only similarity to the man who had been Ryan Brooks were the intense blue eyes. God, the pain of it all; the countless operations, the intensive physiotherapy, rebuilding the shattered shell of his body, the collapse of his entire world, a new face, a new identity, a new life.

And through it all, the one constant source of support, both financial and emotional, was Evelyn. If it hadn't been for her, he would have given up. Ryan Brooks had died in that accident, but Karl Van Ness had been born.

The agony of the past washed over him. Turning upon Ashton suddenly, he grasped her delicate shoulders with his strong hands, eyes afire with ferocity, he searched her face for an answer, and in a voice thick with pain and hurt demanded, 'Where were you?"

Ashton, normally never at a loss for words, was struck dumb for an instant. Eyes filled with compassion, she struggled to understand this unexpected turn of events.

"Where were you?" he repeated.

"I've been right here. I don't understand what you mean."

She watched as the expression in his eyes changed to the deepest yearning she'd ever seen. Were there tears in his eyes or was it the light of this extraordinary place? Before she realized what was happening, his hands slipped to the nape of her neck, entwining themselves in her hair. Almost in the same motion, pulling her to him, she felt the weight of him against her, his lips bruising her mouth with an arrogant possessiveness. As she struggled to free herself she felt her hair, loosed from the French clips by his harsh embrace, cascade down her back.

Shaken by the silken caress of her hair against his hands, he pulled himself away from her, holding her at arm's length, struggling to master his turbulent emotions. Despite her fury, Ashton was grateful he was still holding her; her knees had turned to jelly. He studied her for a moment, his face unreadable. Without a word, he bowed with the faintest gesture of his head, turned on his heel, and walked away.

Ashton remained incredulous, struggling to comprehend the enormity of what had just happened. No one had ever treated her that way. In the space of half an hour she was attracted to, repelled by, and fascinated by, a total stranger. How dare he?

Bombarded by a sea of conflicting emotions she watched as his broad back disappeared into the crowd.

Who did he think he was? In fact — who was he?

Chapter Three

"I see you've met Mr. Van Ness."

Ashton spun around to find herself face to face with a beautiful, elegant woman, leaning casually against the frame of the French doors. It was the woman from the bar.

"What did you say?" gasped Ashton, unable to conceal her shock, and the rising feeling that things were definitely getting out of her control.

"I see you've met Karl Van Ness," repeated the flawless, measured voice.

"That was Karl Van Ness? You mean this is his . . . that was . . ." Ashton vainly gestured in the direction where the stranger had disappeared.

"The very same, my dear." A look of gentle amusement flickered across the intelligent face. Ashton felt the urge to object that she was nobody's dear. It was with considerable effort that she restrained herself, assuming a polite air of nonchalance, attempting to conceal her shock at this latest bombshell.

The woman continued, "And you must be . . . Ashton Cameron."

"How do you know my name?"

Deliberately ignoring her question, Evelyn extended a perfectly manicured hand, "I'm Evelyn, Evelyn St. John. Pleased to meet you, Ashton."

Ashton automatically accepted the hand offered to her. She returned the steady gaze of the dark eyes, so dark they were almost black, nonplussed by the feeling she was being assessed, as only another woman can assess a rival. Ashton didn't know whether to like Evelyn St. John or to distrust her. She scanned the knowing depths of the dark pools, searching for a glimpse of an answer. Did she mistake a hint of warmth there? Why was she the only one here who didn't have the faintest idea about what was happening?

"I believe you dropped these, my dear." Evelyn held out Ashton's hair clips that had dislodged in her unexpected encounter.

"Thank you." She felt like a little girl whose pigtails had just fallen out and someone had stolen her little red wagon.

As Ashton began rearranging her disheveled hair, Evelyn asked quietly, "Will you be staying long?"

"I think I've been here too long already. The sooner I can finish the interview with Mr. Van Ness, the sooner I can leave. I'm sure that will be best for all of us," she said pointedly.

"Don't take it so seriously, Ashton. I know everything is going to be just fine."

Ashton, able to hold her own in any situation, was eager to extricate herself from this uncomfortable conversation. Rather akin to leaving the battle in order to win the war, she thought, although she had no idea how she had inadvertently found herself in a battle. "If you would excuse me, Miss St. John."

"Please call me Evelyn."

"If you don't mind, Evelyn, I'm awfully tired. It's been a very long day, and I think I'll turn in."

As she turned to leave, the softness of Evelyn's voice stopped her. "I suggest, my dear, that you get some rest. You're going to need it."

Just what did she mean by that, thought Ashton, closing the door to her suite behind her. It had been a hell of a trip already, and this was just the first day. Closing the heavy wooden door, she tried to shut out the outside world.

Images of the evening flashed through her mind like a kaleidoscope, the mysterious stranger with those remarkable blue eyes, who as fate would have it just happened to be Karl Van Ness himself, his sophisticated companion, Evelyn? What game was she playing? It was all a bit too strange for words. Ashton believed in the synchronicity of life, that things happened for a reason, that there was no such thing as chance. If she didn't have faith that there was a greater plan to existence, she would have given up long ago. Did a heart ever really heal, she wondered with a sigh?

Too many thoughts were crowding in on her at once. A hot bath would cure her of her analytical tendencies, she decided. Kicking off her shoes, she headed for the luxurious bathroom. With rich, cream colored tile, gold fixtures, and an ornate full length mirror, this was first class treatment. There were definitely advantages to being heiress to one of the largest publishing empires in the United States.

Steam rose from the deep ceramic tub, large enough for two, she noted, as she judiciously added a few drops of vetiver, pine, and lavender into the running water. These oils were precious, like liquid gold.

She reflected with satisfaction on how she had learned what it meant to drive a hard bargain. The richness of the sights and smells like the Palace of Perfume in the shadow of the Egyptian pyramids and the crowded marketplace in Giza. These past years had certainly been quite an education.

Slipping easily out of her evening gown, Ashton sank into the huge tub, sighing appreciatively as the warm soothing waters embraced her, welcoming and comforting. Reclining her head, enjoying the exotic fragrances perfuming the air, she stretched out the length of her long, shapely legs. It was the perfect cure for one of those bizarre days, just what the doctor ordered. Ashton blissfully drifted into her own meditation, content to let the healing waters work their magic.

When she emerged half an hour later, Ashton felt like a new woman. With her spirit newly fortified, the earlier events of the evening seemed somehow unreal, like a bad script from a soap opera. Wrapping herself in a thick white Turkish robe she patted dry the damp ends of her hair that fell just above the curve of her shapely breasts.

She decided to order herself a drink, and to spend some time preparing for her interview with the enigmatic Mr. Van Ness. He certainly did have remarkable charisma and arrogant charm, but she had seen his kind before. She had no intention of becoming another notch on his belt and she would not be caught off guard again. But those blue eyes were enough to unnerve the bravest of hearts, they were so like . . . "Oh stop it, Ashton. Why do you always do this to yourself. Try living in reality for a change," she chided herself.

Reaching for the phone to call room service, Ashton caught sight of an envelope stuffed under the door. A message delivered from the front desk. Now what? Surely not mysterious messages in the night! As her bare feet sunk into the thick pile of the plush carpet, Ashton padded softly to the door. She stood examining the envelope as if it might bite her, trying to fathom its contents, before stooping to collect it.

Sitting on the edge of the bed, she tore it open, breathlessly expectant. It was a fax, a fax from Brent? Brent! Oh my God, Brent. She hadn't given him a second thought after she boarded the plane in New York. Brent. She realized with sudden dismay that she was holding her breath, secretly hoping it was from . . ." Oh, stop being so ridiculous," she told herself. "Why are you obsessing about a man you have just met, and don't even know? You didn't even know his name, till another woman deigned to share it with you."

But what was she going to do about Brent? Reliable,

safe Brent, sending her a message to see if she had arrived safely. She had known him since she was a little girl. They had practically grown up together. His family owns a large chain of department stores across America. Only last year Brent had been promoted to Vice President of the company. He had told her then that all he needed to make him the happiest man alive was for her to marry him.

She smiled fondly, recalling how understanding he had been. He would wait for her, he said. He didn't care how long it took. He loved her. Ashton thought of how supportive Brent had been through all the difficult times. She loved him too, but it was more like what she imagined love for a brother might be, as cliché as that sounded.

He took her to dinner at a great seafood restaurant in Manhattan on the corner of Tenth Avenue and 19th Street just before she left. He reserved a cozy table beside a lovely fire, but Ashton's mind had been a million miles away. He asked her again if she'd made up her heart and her mind. He had only alluded in the briefest way to the ghosts that still haunted her, gently suggesting that it was important to move on with her life.

No, it wasn't healthy to bury herself in her work. She surely didn't need the money. The reins of her father's publishing empire would one day be in her hands, and she certainly knew a great deal already about the operations of the business.

Was it right to settle, though? Should she marry a

man because he was stable, and good, and kind? What about passion? What about romance, love, and fairy tales? Brent, for all his good points, certainly didn't stir in her that indescribable feeling of passion; of not caring about anything else in the world except the person you loved. Her heart didn't leap at the sight of him.

She told him she would make her decision during her time away. She knew from the moment she stepped off the plane that Australia, this land of fire and transformation, was going to change her life. Still deep in thought she picked up the phone. "Hello, this is Ashton Cameron in Room 1305. Yes, I'd like an Absolut martini please, extra dry, three olives."

Chapter Four

Ashton spent the next two hours preparing the outline of the questions she intended for Mr. Van Ness. At least she would have a legitimate reason to interrogate him, she thought amusedly. "Well, Sam, I think that's enough for one night, don't you?" She patted her laptop computer affectionately as she shut it down. They had certainly been through a lot of adventures together.

Pleased with her efforts, she leaned back in the chair, taking a moment to survey the room around her. It really was a beautifully designed space. There was enormous attention to the combination of function and style from the entrance of the small, elegant foyer to the plush sitting room opening onto a full-length balcony.

This space spoke volumes about the taste and mastery of the elusive Mr. Van Ness. Even the dressing area in the bedroom was perfectly designed for a cosmopolitan woman, a very unusual feature in a hotel designed by a man. There was a three-paneled mirror with subtle make-up lighting over a teakwood dressing table with four shallow drawers. It was perfect.

How many times had Ashton found herself trying to apply makeup in sadly inadequate light in some of the best hotels in the world. Despite her mixed feelings, Mr. Van Ness obviously had an innate sense of harmony, balance, and a woman's needs.

Leaving her almost untouched martini, Ashton slipped out of the cuddly robe and put on her favorite pearl grey nightgown. The bias cut silk hugged her every curve, making her feel warm and safe, even though with its low back and fine straps, the effect was anything but safe.

Plumping up two of the huge down pillows, she slipped between the fine, scented sheets. Sleep came almost immediately.

The smell of sea air filled her nostrils, and the light seemed to be changing. Swimming in the clear, aqua depths, the water warm and gentle against her nakedness, Ashton was absolutely at peace. The eerie light and fluid shapes signaled that she was in a netherworld, a cocoon of both sound and silence. She was aware of being lifted by enormously strong arms, cradled almost like a tiny child, with water running in rivulets down her bare skin.

The sand squeaked under the firm steps of the man who carried her. Yes, it was a man. She knew that, though she couldn't quite see his face. She was safe. Carried through a labyrinth of corridors open to the sea, his heartbeat was like a soothing drum against her ear.

A door magically opened, and the strong arms laid her gently upon silken pillows, covering her with a soft robe. A shadow passed over her closed eyes as he lowered his face to hers. The combination of strength and tenderness of his mouth plumbed the very core of her. She could taste the salt on his skin and smell the ocean in his thick hair. The kiss was endless, timeless, and familiar.

Her eyes flew open. Ashton sat upright, disoriented in her unfamiliar surroundings. God, it was only a dream. She felt so safe, so happy. Tears welled in her eyes. Furious with herself, she leapt out of bed. It was 2 AM! Well, she was not going to sit here all night tormenting herself.

Slipping into a one piece maillot that somehow still managed to leave nothing to the imagination, she flung on the Turkish robe, monogrammed with the O of the Osprey Hotel, and headed to the rooftop pool. Ashton was relieved not to meet anyone at this insane hour of the morning.

Discarding her robe, she dove cleanly into the cool water, and began systematically swimming laps, determined to dispel her jumbled feelings. Her muscles, like her whole frame, were fine, long, and lithe. Ashton had a slender, but voluptuous body. Her strokes cutting the water cleanly, she completed four laps without a hint of effort, barely raising her pulse.

Supporting herself at the edge of the pool, she leaned back and gazed up at the night sky, scattered with stardust. They're different, she thought, and how incredibly. . . .

"That's the Southern Cross."

Ashton jumped at the sound of the amused voice. She nearly swallowed half the pool. She turned to find those riveting blue eyes appraising her over the top of a crystal glass.

"How long have you been here?" she sputtered.

"Long enough."

"Well I certainly hope you enjoyed the show."

He gave her his most charming smile, which made her want to hit him with a shoe, if only she had one with her.

"I suppose you come here to survey your guests' swimming habits at night?" she asked caustically.

"Actually, I come here to look at the Southern Cross."

Ashton suddenly felt very exposed, aware of his burning gaze catching the outline of her nipples pushing against the all too thin wet fabric.

"You must be cold." He offered his hand to help her out of the pool.

"I can manage, thank you."

Holding out her robe, his mocking tone changed to one of sincere warmth. "Please forgive me, Ashton. My behavior this evening was abominable."

He enfolded her in the robe, his arms remaining around her for just the slightest instant too long. She felt the urge to cut him to pieces with words, but something in his eyes stopped her. "All right, Mr. Van Ness. Let's call a truce."

Offering to seal the pact, she extended her hand. Tenderly he accepted it, bowed slightly like a 17th century courtier, and grazed the back of her hand with the faintest whisper of his warm breath. His lips never touched her skin and as his blazing eyes locked with hers, he murmured, "I'd like that, I'd like that very much."

Ashton felt as though her hand had been branded. The pit of her stomach was in turmoil, and she felt sure he could see her heart pounding; any harder and it would leap right out of her chest.

"Why didn't you tell me who you were?" she asked, vainly trying to hide her emotional state.

"You took me by surprise."

"What do you mean by that?"

"You're a very beautiful woman, Ashton. Surely I'm not the first man to be captivated by your charms."

Smiling despite herself, she said, "I wasn't trying to captivate anyone."

"With that dress you were wearing? Liar!" He laughed — a deep, warm, resonant laugh. "Since we're going to be great friends why don't you start by telling me a little about yourself."

Great friends! And just what did he mean by that?

"You don't waste time, do you?"

"Never. Life is far too fleeting and time far too precious."

"It sounds like you've learned that the hard way." Ashton searched his face for a hint of an answer. He merely smiled, shaking his head gently.

"You get your chance to ask questions tomorrow."

"So you agree? You'll really let me do a feature on you?" Ashton, she admonished herself, you sound like a silly schoolgirl!

"On one condition only." A hint of mischief danced in his blue eyes.

Not at all sure she would like the answer, Ashton couldn't help but ask, "And what might that be?"

"I have two tickets to the opera tomorrow night. I would like it very much if you would join me."

The opera. Did he have any idea how much she loved it — the soaring music, passion, and drama; it spoke to her very soul.

"Wouldn't you rather take Evelyn?" Ashton wished she hadn't said it even before the words had left her mouth. Where did that remark come from? "How could you be so ungracious, Ashton," she chided herself. Karl just stood looking at her with the faintest hint of mirth on his face, eyes full of laughter, at her unexpected outburst.

Apologetically she continued, "I'm sorry, that was rude of me." Attempting to salvage the situation she added gaily, "You drive a hard bargain. I would love to see the opera with you."

"Curtain is at 7:30 PM. Be at my suite by 5:00 and we can take care of business first. That will leave plenty of time for pleasure."

Ignoring his last remark Ashton extended her hand, "I look forward to it, Mr. Van Ness."

"Karl," he corrected, bending to kiss her hand yet again. Turning it palm up he planted a searing kiss at its delicate center. Ashton felt a barely perceptible tremor begin in the pit of her stomach. She was rendered totally immobile by the conflicting passions he was stirring. As if sensing her inability or unwillingness to move he nuzzled, kissed and fondled her hand and fingers, making love to her.

Ashton involuntarily stepped closer, closer to the source of this delicious torment. She ached to grab his hair with both her hands and kiss his mouth until they both couldn't breathe. Pulse racing, warning bells clamoring loudly, she wanted him to kiss all of her that same way, every part of her. . . .

Mustering every ounce of self-discipline she possessed, she pulled her hand from his touch and murmured shakily, "Until tomorrow then."

Chapter Five

Karl, aflame with desire, watched as her feminine curves disappeared through the doorway. "Don't go, darling," he whispered, but he was standing alone.

Taking up his scotch again from the poolside table, Karl examined the contents of his glass, deep in thought. Ten years was a long time. He had never thought he would see her again, especially not here at the other end of the world. Reclining on a deck chair, gazing at the Southern Cross, he wondered how it was possible to have been through so much and survived.

His mind went back to the day that had altered his destiny forever. They had been so in love, or so he thought. Her parents weren't thrilled by their declaration of love, had spoken of the folly of youth, of waiting a few more years, but they had decided their own course. Karl remembered how he had waited for her in the rain that night, how his heart leapt at the sight of her, carrying a small duffel bag, running towards him in a clinging, sodden dress, laughing.

They had arranged for a little service in Elkton, Maryland. They could be married in a flash, no waiting. It would only take two days. They would be married before anyone could do anything about it.

They were almost there when tragedy struck. He didn't see the out-of-control bus rounding the tight bend until too late. The greasy, rain slicked road afforded no assistance as he fought in vain to avert disaster. There was no place to go. Karl grimaced as he recalled clutching Ashton's hand in that final moment, the sound of the initial impact and screaming metal, as their car ploughed into the hurtling bus.

His next recollection was of awakening in a hospital bed, his body awash in a sea of pain. Face masked in bandages, jaw wired shut, he was immobilized in traction. Beside his bed sat not Ashton, but Evelyn, leaning earnestly towards him, loving and concerned. What was Evelyn doing here?

Evelyn, recently widowed, was wealthy, sophisticated, and educated, the wife of his former Dean. She told him he possessed an exceptional talent, a gift for architecture that would make him one of the greats. She knew he had no family, no support network, but she believed in him. She had vowed to help him.

Evelyn told him his accident had been near fatal. He was in a coma for almost a week. The impact hurled him through the windshield, he had suffered serious multiple injuries and hadn't been expected to survive. The best surgeons worked to piece him back together. His face was destroyed. The surgeons were going to reconstruct it with the best technology available at Evelyn's insistence and expense.

Karl remembered how, as she was talking, he had frantically searched the room before staring panic-stricken at Evelyn for an answer. She understood. Yes, she had survived, Evelyn nodded. Survived! Thank God! He wanted to scream with joy, but every inch of him throbbed with pain he had never imagined a human could feel.

Evelyn avoided his gaze, searching her face for answers. She wanted him to rest but his pleading eyes demanded she continue. Evelyn sighed resignedly and told him what he would eventually have to know. Know what, he wondered.

Yes, Ashton was alive and miraculously had escaped relatively unscathed. And then came the words that made him wish he had died that night. Evelyn had looked him in the eyes and in her quiet voice told him that Ashton had left for Europe, that she wasn't coming back He didn't understand at first, couldn't comprehend what she had told him. She had to repeat it to him several times for it to sink in. Ashton had left him. Like this? At his moment of greatest need? Evelyn told him how sorry she was.

He didn't want to be consoled; he wished he had died. And during the following days, weeks, and months of hurt and rage, that was when he had made his decision. He would fight. He would live. Determined to recover, he resolved to become a new person and assume a new identity. He would be successful and powerful, and no one, no one would be in a position to hurt him in this way again.

Ten years. He had truly become a new person in that time. Evelyn had been with him every step of the way. Her encouragement, love, and support had helped him through the endless follow-up operations. The new Karl Van Ness was nothing like his former self, Ryan Brooks.

His new face was a testament to modem technology and the skill and artistry of the surgeon's hand

The intensive rehabilitation reshaped his body. He had been attractive and with average muscular definition; now his body was hardened and well-defined from hours and months of swimming and weightlifting. Even his voice had deepened and changed as a result of the trauma suffered. For all intents, Ryan had been reborn.

Karl got up and strolled to the railing. Sydney's distinctive skyline sprawled before him. Success had come at a huge price. What was he to do now with this unexpected ghost from his past? She had only become more beautiful, more confident, and more self-assured. She had blossomed into a truly beautiful woman! She was a journalist now. She had no idea who he really was. She was attracted to him, despite herself, he knew. She had loved him and left him.

He thought that he had let go of the anger long ago, but her sudden reappearance conjured up memories of the torment and pain of the accident . . . of life without her. She had been so vulnerable, so loving, so caring. How could he have been so wrong? Was he wrong? Should he reveal himself? No, not yet. What to do?

As the first rays of the sun broke over the horizon, Karl smiled to himself as the idea dawned upon him. Ashton Cameron, he vowed, I'm going to wine you, dine you, and romance you like no man has ever done. I'm going to make love to you day and night. I'm going to teach you a lesson.

Chapter Six

Ashton rolled over and pulled the covers closer, trying to shut out the incessant banging. In her sleep-warm state the dull sound continued to nag her, demanding attention. Opening her bleary eyes to take stock of her surroundings, she realized that it was not her head that was pounding but someone knocking on the door to her suite. Glancing at the bedside clock Ashton groaned, 8:30 AM. Who could it be at this hour?

Reluctantly slipping out of her warm cocoon, Ashton donned her robe, and somehow, in a half-asleep daze groggily made her way to the door. Again, the firm knock. "Who is it?" she mumbled, scarcely able to conceal her annoyance at being awakened.

"Room service."

Room service? Puzzled, Ashton opened the door only to be greeted by a smiling waiter wheeling a trolley laden with what she supposed was breakfast, but looked more like a three course dinner, complete with a bottle of chilled champagne. "But I didn't order this."

"Compliments of Mr. Van Ness, Madam. May I?"

"Oh . . . yes. Of course." Ashton stepped out of the doorway, allowing him a clear path to wheel the banquet into her suite.

"Will it be all right here, Madam?" he asked, pausing in the living area. He looked slightly amused by her obvious surprise.

"Yes, thank you," replied Ashton.

"Not at all, Madam."

Ashton was in the process of reaching for some loose change on the counter when the waiter interjected, "That won't be necessary. When you're finished just dial room service and someone will be along to collect the trolley." He smiled at her politely and saw himself out.

Ashton watched him leave, reminding herself that of course tipping was not a custom in this part of the world . . . hard to remember when it was such an ingrained habit.

Turning back to the laden trolley she was struck by the color and style of the presentation of tropical fruits — mango, pineapple, strawberries, and kiwi. She smiled as the unmistakable aroma of eggs Florentine greeted her as she lifted the silver cover from the hot dish — her favorite. How did he guess?

There was an assortment of breads, croissants, and bagels, with every sort of jam imaginable. There was enough food for ten people, she thought, resolving that the Veuve Clicquot Rosé chilling in a silver ice bucket would have to wait till later. Resting against the sole champagne flute was an envelope, simply addressed in a beautiful, bold hand, to Ashton.

Heart fluttering in anticipation, Ashton opened the note and quickly scanned the contents. In the same black ink, obviously that of a fountain pen, was written 5:00 PM sharp, Suite 2010 — Karl. Ashton stared at the note incredulously, vaguely disappointed. That's it? He sends me all of this and that's all he writes.

He really was a most unusual man and had obviously had a great deal of practice charming the ladies. Too much practice! Was this just one of his tactics? Why was he so strange last night? What was the incident on the balcony all about? One minute he was utterly attentive and charming, and the next so distant. And that kiss! She had been outraged by his audacity, but it had been years since she had been kissed like that. Correction, she had never been kissed like that. She almost hadn't wanted him to stop.

Ashton looked at the breakfast laid out before her. There really was no point in standing there obsessing about his possible intentions and letting perfectly good eggs Florentine get cold! Her father had always been proud of her sense of practicality. No surprise really, since she had inherited it from him. She would get her chance to ask Karl Van Ness questions later, at 5:00 PM sharp!

It was nearly 11:00 AM by the time Ashton had showered, applied some light makeup, and slipped into her casual pant suit. The rich creamy silk made her complexion glow and the simple elegance of the wrap jacket flattered her perfect figure. Her classic alligator pumps, that rich Ferragamo brown, completed her outfit.

By the time room service returned to collect the trolley, there wasn't that much to collect. Ashton had been hungrier than she realized and had acquitted herself admirably. If the waiter was surprised, he did well to conceal his wonder.

It was a glorious day as Ashton thanked the concierge and stepped into a taxi. She had decided to spend some of the day exploring the delights of Sydney. It really was perfect weather for some sightseeing: a clear blue sky, clean air, and such an unusual quality of light, quite unlike any other part of the world she had visited.

She spent the next few hours enchanted by the delights of the historic Rocks area, Darling Harbour, and Circular Quay where she saw a replica of the Endeavour, the ship sailed by Captain Cook when he discovered Botany Bay in 1788. As she admired the city around her, Ashton almost found it hard to believe that all of it had started off as a penal colony for the British. It certainly lent the place a character and unique flavor all its own.

It was mid-afternoon by the time Ashton casually strolled back into the foyer of the Osprey Hotel. She noted the feeling of tranquility bestowed by the marble floors, the many lush plants and the indoor central pond. The effect was made complete by the waterfall cascading down the central column that housed the elevators. "An ingenious use of space," she thought appreciatively.

Approaching the reception desk she was greeted by the same petite blonde woman who had helped her check in. "Hi, Linda. Are there any messages for 1305?"

Punching a button on the screen before her, the young woman smiled and shook her head, "No messages, Ms. Cameron."

"Thanks." Ashton was relieved as she headed for her suite. She was glad for the chance to relax for a while and compose herself before her encounter with Karl. He unnerved her more than she liked to admit.

Sliding her card into the electronic lock, Ashton stopped dead in her tracks as the door swung open. Utterly amazed by the scene that greeted her, she made herself check the number on the door just to be sure she was in the right room. 1305, yes, this was her suite.

Mouth agape with astonishment and delight, Ashton walked into her suite filled to overflowing with roses. At least ten huge bouquets of every variety of rose imaginable filled the room — beautiful white roses with sprigs of baby's breath, red roses, yellow roses, coral pink roses. They were exquisite, perfuming the air with a heady, exotic aroma. "My God," she thought, "they're absolutely fabulous! Who on earth would do such a thing?"

Ashton cast her eyes over the scene in wonder, searching for the sign of a card or any other hint at the fairy godmother. There was nothing — not a note slipped under the door or on the desk. There were no cards on any of the bouquets. Perplexed, she picked up the phone, dialing reception.

A woman's voice answered, "Osprey Hotel; Linda speaking."

"Linda, it's Ashton Cameron again. Are you absolutely sure there are no messages?"

There was a brief pause before Linda replied, "Sorry, Ms. Cameron. I'm absolutely positive. I'll let you know if anything comes in."

"Thanks for your trouble, Linda."

"Anytime, Ms. Cameron."

Ashton gently replaced the receiver as she sat on the couch. It had to be Brent, she mused. No doubt he was subtly trying to encourage an answer of "yes," if you could consider a room full of roses subtle. It really was awfully sweet of him.

He truly surprised her this time. Just when she thought him thoroughly predictable. For him to do something so wonderfully outrageous and romantic just took the cake. Maybe she really would grow to love him after all. Still, she had no intention of being romanced into a marriage she wasn't certain about.

Chapter Seven

Glancing at the desk clock, Ashton realized that she had less than two hours to get herself together for the interview and her night at the opera. She would have to give Brent a thank you call later. At least she didn't have to think about what she would wear to the opera that night. She knew she had just the perfect gown.

Ashton had just stepped into her bias-cut silk gown. Its lustrous fabric was a fascinating combination of bronze and copper hues that subtly accentuated her every curve.

She was draping the matching Fortuny pleated wrap around her bare shoulders when her phone rang. Maybe it was her father checking on her progress, she mused, fastening her coral earrings, "Hello."

"Ashton honey, how are you?"

"Brent! Hi, I'm just fine."

"Did you have a good flight? Did you get my fax? Are you well? What's it like there?"

Ashton laughed, he was just like a big kid sometimes, asking so many questions at once. "Well in that order the answers are, yes, yes, I'm doing fine, and I love it here. Thanks so much for your fax, I didn't expect to hear from you so soon."

"You don't think I going to let my girl escape to the antipodes, do you?"

"Brent, I'm not your girl," she corrected.

"Yet," he added, oblivious to the obvious tolerance in Ashton's voice.

She didn't want to encourage him when she had reached no decision. In fact, she hadn't really given the question of marrying him any serious thought at all, but she had to thank him for the flowers. It really would be rude not to mention them, and futile to try and avoid the issue.

"Brent, thanks for the roses. They're gorgeous. The room is overflowing. Really, it's awfully extravagant of you, I love them. Whatever possessed you to send them?"

Dead silence.

"Brent? Brent, are you there?"

When he finally answered his voice was a mixture of embarrassment and confusion. "Ashton honey . . . I didn't send you any roses."

"You didn't?" She almost choked in amazement. "Then . . . but . . . they're so beautiful, and . . ."

Awkwardly he repeated, "I didn't send any roses."

"Oh! But I was so sure they were from you. Come on Brent, stop joking, be serious now."

His voice struggling to conceal a hint of anger, he continued, "I'm quite serious, unfortunately. What's going on there, Ashton? Who's sending you flowers?"

And breakfast, and champagne she thought, before quipping lightly, "I guess I must have a secret admirer!"

"Well, I'm not sure I like it! When are you coming home?"

"Oh, stop it, Brent. I just got here, and I have work to do. Which reminds me I have to dash or I'll be late."

"Late for what?"

"We'll have to talk later, Brent, I've got to go. I'll call you tonight after the opera. . ."

"Opera? Who are you going to the op . . . ?"

"Thanks for the call, Brent, I'll talk to you later, okay? Bye."

"Yeah, bye."

Oops, Ashton thought, as she hung up the phone, that was a bad faux pas. Pull that foot out of your mouth. Looking at the roses again, she smiled thinking of Karl — it hadn't occurred to her they could have been from him. Two rather extravagant gifts in one day, and she had only just met him. He was certainly moving fast, but then it was plainly obvious that there was nothing mediocre or ordinary about him.

Adding the final touches to her makeup, Ashton checked herself in the full-length mirror, pleased by the elegant yet sensual image that greeted her. Yes, this would do quite nicely. Gathering up her miniature tape recorder and clutch purse she glided out of the apartment with five minutes to spare. It was going to be quite an interview.

The door to his suite was slightly ajar when she arrived. Glancing at her watch the gold hands showed 5:00 PM. He was obviously waiting for her. She knocked lightly, waiting for a response. No answer. "Hello, Karl? It's me, Ashton." She waited hesitantly for a moment, deciding whether to venture in.

Oh go on, she thought, he's obviously left the door open for you. Pushing the door, she cautiously walked into his suite. She would normally not have been so bold, but logic told her it was all right considering he had been so particular about her being on time.

His suite was more like an apartment. Decorated in natural hues, it was a tasteful combination of creme, teak and a deep forest green. It suited him perfectly, as if it had been made for him; but then he was the designer, wasn't he?

Ashton could hear the sound of conversation and laughter coming from the living area. Karl's unmistakably husky voice was mingled with that of a woman's. Curiosity burned in Ashton's veins. She wasn't about to stand around in the hallway waiting to be summoned; it was bad enough that she had shown up exactly on time. Mustering every ounce of feminine grace and charm in her svelte frame, Ashton casually strolled into the living room.

Karl, dressed in a rich maroon velvet dressing gown, was with his back to her, leaning attentively over a woman seated on the lounge. She should have known it would be Evelyn.

Ashton watched as he finished fastening the clasp on what appeared to be a very real and expensive glittering necklace. No chance of those rocks being cubic zirconia, she mused.

Ashton felt the heat rising in her face as she watched him whisper something in Evelyn's ear, making her laugh, before kissing her lightly on the cheek. Feeling like an unwanted appendage, Ashton was just deciding that this visit was perhaps not the wisest of ideas, when he turned and saw her.

"Hello, Ashton. We didn't hear you come in." He flashed his devastatingly handsome smile.

Oooh, but he was good looking. Ashton knew from the bronzed bare skin of his chest showing through the opening of his gown, that he was naked beneath it. She caught herself wondering what he would look like without it. She hoped she wasn't blushing.

Forcing herself to sound coherent she retorted, "No, obviously you didn't. Forgive me for barging in, but the door was open, and you did say 5:00 PM sharp. I'm sorry, I didn't mean to interrupt. . . ."

Chapter Eight

"You're not interrupting anything, my dear," purred Evelyn, rising to her feet. "I was just on my way out."

"Ashton, you've met Evelyn?" Karl gestured between the two women.

"Yes, I've had the pleasure." Ashton nodded politely.

Turning to Karl, Evelyn kissed him gently on the cheek, "You two have a wonderful time." She paused before adding pointedly, "I'll see you later." And with that, she picked up her bag, cast Ashton a knowing look, turned and glided out of the room.

Ashton was left standing alone with Karl. "Sorry about that," he offered. "There was some unfinished business to take care of."

Ashton shot back quickly, "Really? And you always do business dressed like that I suppose?"

"Only when I intend to mix it with pleasure," he smiled, his blue eyes twinkling with mischief.

When he looked at her like that it was impossible to be angry with him. "Thank you for the breakfast." He bowed gallantly in his best cavalier fashion.

Ashton felt a rush of delight, she added, "And the flowers, they're beautiful. But you shouldn't have."

"Why not?"

His question surprised her, she hadn't really thought why not, just that nobody had before. Searching for a response, she blurted, "But I hardly know you."

Voice soft and full of implication, he asked quietly, "Can you think of a better way to get to know me?" She was aware of his gaze traveling the length of her, eyes darkening with smoky intensity. He murmured huskily, "My God, Ashton, you are beautiful."

Her pulse quickened as he stepped closer to her, placing his arms about her waist, "I'm glad you're here," he whispered almost inaudibly. He was studying her face intently, as if trying to commit every feature to memory. Closing his eyes, he gently caressed her cheek with his, drinking in the fragrance of her hair.

Ashton thought she was going to melt in his embrace. She felt her knees ready to buckle despite her best efforts to keep a tight rein over her racing emotions. "Karl, what about the interview?" she whispered in vain, distracted by his breath on her earlobe.

As his solid, bare chest pressed against her, she had to fight to restrain herself from running her fingers through its thick dark tangle of curls. She was all too aware that his robe was the only thing separating her from the rest of him, vital and present.

"Karl, I didn't come here to make love to you," Ashton protested.

His lips tenderly sought out hers, kissing her with a strength and gentleness that made her think she would lose her mind. She found herself responding to him, her body molding itself to his, as he deepened the kiss, exploring the soft inner flesh of her lips with his tongue. Clutching his shoulders, her fingers reached to entangle themselves in the dark curls at the nape of his neck. She wanted this sensation to last forever. She felt alive for the first time in years.

She was rescued from the tide that was beginning to sweep her away as he drew back from her, the effort of his self-control evident in his face. Looking at her bewildered expression, he rasped, "Are you sure about that, Ashton?"

Not altogether in command of her faculties, she gasped uncomprehendingly, "What?" his meaning slowly dawning upon her.

Their eyes locked in an unspoken challenge. He had made his intentions quite clear, but Ashton had no interest in being just another conquest. Taking a moment to catch her breath, she added in the most businesslike manner she could manage, "Shall we get on with the interview?"

His blue eyes twinkled with a mixture of admiration and amusement. "As you wish. Would you excuse me while I get dressed first?"

Ashton nodded.

"Good. Make yourself at home. I won't be long."

Ashton watched as he disappeared into the bedroom without so much as a backward glance. He was so perplexing. There was such tenderness concealed in the depths of those flashing blue eyes. There was also something so familiar in those eyes, almost as if she knew him, though she had never met anyone like him before.

Glancing about the room, she committed every tiny detail to memory, eager to know more about him. There was classical music playing softly. A very distinctive bottle of Dalwhinne scotch, in the company of a Baccarat crystal ice bucket, sat on the black marble bar. In the far comer was a desk, covered with papers, and rolled tubes of plan skins. Adjacent to the desk, in front of the French doors opening onto the huge terrace, there was a drafting board set up. This suite had obviously become office and home for quite a while.

Ashton slowly walked about the room, inhaling the scent of the man. A scent that recalled . . . and then there was Evelyn's perfume. Her fingers trailed absently over the raw silk of the couch, as she wondered what production he was taking her to see. She hadn't even bothered to ask. Her eyes caught sight of an Australian Opera brochure tossed casually on his desk. Yielding to the urge to satisfy her boundless curiosity, she wandered over for a closer look.

La Traviata? Oh, how absolutely perfect. Verdi was one of her favorite composers. It was going to be a wonderful evening of music. Lying next to the brochure was an elegant fountain pen. Ashton picked it up, feeling its perfect balance in her hand. Mont Blanc. He had elegant taste.

She giggled to herself wondering if he perhaps had any fashion tragedies secreted away in the closet. She could just imagine a lovely crocheted homemade doily collection from Aunt Mae locked away from the style police. God, but she had a twisted sense of humor sometimes!

Replacing the pen, she couldn't help but notice a message lying carelessly atop a pile of documents. In spite of herself, the words darling and Paris leapt off the page at her . . . Karl, darling, Paris is a bore without you. I'm waiting.

Ashton couldn't bear to read anymore. How many women did he have falling all over him? It was silly to be jealous, and yet the chain of events that had transpired in the past 24 hours gave her a sense of a relationship developing. She avoided relationships for years. Was she out of her mind to be harboring hopes of something serious? The champagne, the roses — wasn't it all just a game to him? Hadn't he done the same to countless women before her? Damn it, Ashton, stop asking so many questions and enjoy the present.

"Okay, I'm all yours."

Ashton turned to find him standing in the bedroom doorway, adjusting the cuffs of his dinner jacket, bcaming at her. As her best friend Julie would exclaim, he was drop dead gorgeous.

"Where do you want me?" he continued in the same leading fashion.

Doing her best to ignore the intonation, Ashton pointed to the couch, "Here's fine."

When they were both seated and Ashton set her tape recorder running, she began. "I really appreciate you taking the time for this, Karl."

He nodded acknowledgment.

"You're being hailed as one of the most talented

architects of the twenty-first century. How do you feel about having such expectations placed upon you?"

He smiled, thinking for a moment before replying, "You know, the public is a very fickle animal. What they love today, they may reject tomorrow on a whim. It happens. I think Shakespeare sums up my philosophy best when he says, 'To thine own self be true.'"

"What do you mean?"

"Well, you can't spend your life worrying about what other people think Do what you do with all your heart. Be the very best you know you can be. It doesn't matter whether you clean houses, drive a taxi, or perform brain surgery."

She hadn't expected a response like that. She continued, "How is it that a man as successful as yourself has hardly been interviewed? You know, I couldn't even find a picture of what you looked like."

"Does it really matter what I look like? I want my work, my designs, to speak for who I am. I don't think the fact that Karl Van Ness has a handsome face is going to change things."

"Change what things?"

"The way people see the world, or the way people treat the world. I like beautiful things," he cocked an appreciative eyebrow in Ashton's direction, "And if I can help the world be a better place, because of the way I work, then I'm serving a purpose."

"What about family? Are they a source of support and inspiration for you?" She was aware of his hawk-like gaze upon her, assessing how to answer her. "I have no family."

"No attachments?" she asked lightly, her manner completely at odds with the sudden rush of her heart. He shook his head very deliberately, "No attachments."

Ashton bit her tongue, wondering if that meant Evelyn too.

Still studying her, he added, "Ashton, when is your deadline for this article?"

"I have till the end of next week."

"Good, why don't we stop the interrogation right now. I have a better idea."

"And just what might that be?"

"Spend some time with me over the next few days. It will give us a chance to get to know each other a lot better, and you can slip in the odd question. I really don't like formal interviews, you know."

"Well, I . . .I guess that would be all right." When Ashton thought about the possibility of spending more time with him, she felt like a kid playing with fire.

"Great . . . that's settled then." He stood, extending a hand to help her up, "I have a reservation for us at the Fountain Room in 20 minutes. I thought you might like something to eat, before the show."

As he escorted her from the room on his arm, Ashton had the distinct feeling that he had skillfully maneuvered just the outcome he wanted; he had it all planned!

"I won't stay, Karl, I just want to pick up my tape recorder."

Karl closed the door behind them. Ashton couldn't remember when she had enjoyed an evening more. He had been the perfect gentleman, attentive, funny, charming.

They made a beautiful couple, as one little old lady had stopped to tell them, as they were climbing the steps to the main entrance of the opera house.

The Sydney Opera House was an experience. What an amazing design and concept for such a building. *La Traviata* was a sensational production. Ashton had cried openly in the final scene as Alfredo reached the dying Violetta's bedside. For Alfredo to discover that Violetta had left him only to appease his father, and because she loved him. What a tragedy! Did life really imitate art? It sure seemed that way.

Walking to the bar where Karl was pouring himself a drink, she handed his silk handkerchief back to him. "Thank you," she said softly.

Looking into her eyes, searching her very soul, he took her gently by the hand and led her to the couch. "What is it, Ashton? What ghost haunts you so?"

"What makes you think I'm haunted by ghosts," she blinked, trying hard to stem a new flood of tears that threatened to spring forth. She would not have the excuse of a tragic opera to save her this time.

"I saw the way you cried. I'm not sure it was only because of the music."

"Karl, there are some things I just don't want to talk about." She could hear the words from the first act: *Ah, forse lui che l'anima*. Perhaps it is he, who, when my soul was lonely and troubled, used to tint it with invisible colors . . .She thought back to that tragic night ten years ago as the tears began to stream down her face.

Placing his arms about her, he held her tenderly as she sobbed. She felt like a child in his arms, as she clutched his neck, her body racked by the pain and sorrow of all that she had tried to contain.

"Ashton, darling, you're safe," he whispered as he rocked her. "It's okay." He held her silently then, waiting for her sobs to subside.

"Karl," she whispered.

He flinched at the sound of pain and fragility in her voice. "Yes, Ashton." He was gently brushing her face with the back of his fingers.

"Karl," she whispered, "I want you to make love to me."

She saw his jaw tense. She had not expected to hear herself say such a thing, but enough was enough. She wasn't going to be a prisoner to her past any longer.

"Ashton," he groaned, burying his face in her hair. "Are you sure it's what you want?" Raw desire thickened his voice.

She nodded and repeated, "Make love to me, Karl, right here, right now"

"No, not here," he whispered, his voice hoarse with desire. He lifted her easily in his arms and carried her into the bedroom.

Chapter Nine

Karl roughly pushed aside the pillows as he tugged back the covers of the king-sized bed. Placing Ashton gently on the bed, he stood back from her, eyes ablaze, struggling to control his ragged breathing and the ache in his loins. She lay with her fiery hair spread across the pillow, her face a mixture of innocence, yearning, and apprehension.

She stretched her arms out to him in invitation. A groan from the depths of his being escaped his lips as he lowered himself beside her, gazing into her soft grey-green eyes, a window to the very center of her soul.

"Ashton . . ." he whispered.

She raised her fingers to the softness of his lips, preventing him from finishing. Tilting her face slightly, she began kissing the hard line of his jaw, the corners of his mouth. The warmth of his breath brushed her face as he slowly lowered his mouth with a delicious deliberateness, to meet her own. Their lips met in a kiss that was timeless, endless, and Ashton felt herself carried on a tide of desire that shook her to her very core.

Hands trembling, she tugged at his shirt as he shrugged his jacket off, tossing it carelessly to the floor. Sliding her hands up under his shirt, he groaned as her delicate fingers explored his muscular back, savoring the contact with his flesh, aching to feel more of him closer to her.

He began kissing her neck, her shoulders, following the plunging neckline of her gown with burning lips. Her nipples strained against the thin silk as he teased them with his strong fingers. She felt the warm wetness between her thighs, the female scent of her surrounding them. His dark head bent to kiss the hollow of her hip; her hands locked in his hair willing him to continue, to take her, to erase all the pain of the past. The hunger she felt for him amazed her, it was as though she had been asleep and was only now beginning to awaken. A trembling began deep inside, her pulse was racing. The world of order, of reason, no longer mattered — she needed to see his eyes.

With all her heart she needed to tell him — to explain. "Karl, darling. . ." her face was aflame with desire, with shyness. . .

"Karl, look at me, please look at me." Her breath came in ragged gasps, "I don't know why I want you so. . . I haven't been able to forget . . . I haven't let anyone . . ."

The gentleness in his eyes and the tender way he was holding her shoulders was too much for Ashton. Suddenly it seemed as though the armor she had built so carefully and polished so faithfully was lying at her feet, and for the first time in her life, she felt truly naked.

She felt the hot tears rising and tried vainly to stem their flow, but his gentle hands stroked her hair and his gaze never wavered from hers. All the tears she had never shed all those years ago overflowed and her body was racked with sobs. She cried as she never had, and all the while his strong arms held her, rocking her gently. When she tried to speak she found she couldn't, and the tears began anew.

The scent of him soothed her and the beating of his heart was like a caress. His arms enfolded her and the warmth of his hard body curled protectively around her. He murmured her name and the last thing she thought she heard him say was, "How I loved you." But that didn't make sense, she thought sleepily.

"What did you say, Karl?"

"Nothing, sweet one, just that you are safe, I'm here."

"You won't let me go?" Her voice was tiny, soft . . .

"No darling, I won't let you go."

The sun streamed through the open blinds, bathing the room with the softness of early morning light. Ashton sat up slowly. Did anyone get the number of that bus, she wondered. She felt like she'd been run over and that it had backed up over her just for good measure.

A sudden rush of panic washed over her as she realized that the reason the sheets felt so silken smooth against her skin was because she was stark naked. Her stomach sank as it slowly dawned on her where she was and whose bed she was in! Clutching the covers about her she sat struggling to make sense of the jumble of images from the night before.

Oh God, did I really say all those things, she wondered? She groaned as she spotted her evening gown draped over a chair in the comer of the room, her shoes placed neatly beside it. She had been praying that she had dreamed last night. No such luck!

And to make matters worse she didn't even have the poor comfort of having been tipsy. How on earth did she manage to find herself in such a situation?

She was almost afraid to look at the pillow beside her. Expecting to see Karl's sleeping form next to her, she turned to discover the imprint of where he had been. In his place lay a single red rose with a small note beside it.

It read very simply — Ashton. My arms are still around you. You're beautiful when you sleep. Have been called away on business. How about dinner tomorrow night? Karl.

Ashton glowed with pleasure despite her apprehension. Karl was so attentive. She smiled ruefully. In spite of her emotional state last night, he had been the perfect gentleman. It really was most curious that she allowed her defenses to slip when she had struggled so hard to maintain them for all these years. But something in Karl's being spoke to her, called to her soul. It was more than the physical attraction.

And yet Ashton had amazed even herself at the desire she had felt for him. Somehow, she had managed to convince herself that she could live without physical intimacy; that her career and her insanely busy lifestyle could fill the void in her heart left by Ryan's death. How strange it was to discover these powerful yearnings now forcing their way to the surface of her consciousness. The suppressed feelings were now clamoring, demanding to be honored . . . and to be healed.

Her honesty in admitting her own feelings had been a major step for her. It was frightening, and yet somehow what had occurred between them was important and right. Ashton smiled, recalling how tenderly he had held her. He hadn't asked questions; his arms had given her the haven she craved — allowing her to express the grief she had been denying. He had put his own desire aside, restraining his ardent passion. He had been supportive of her — giving, not just taking — like so many men she had met who were eager to seize what they assumed was rightfully theirs.

She chuckled as she visualized what an unromantic moment it must have been — one instant the two of them afire, racing towards fulfillment, an explosion of passion, and the next her falling asleep in his arms like a baby, emotionally exhausted. He must have had quite a time getting her out of the gown without any assistance.

As she dressed, Ashton looked about the room. The smell of Karl's aftershave hung thick in the air. She had been far too preoccupied last night to notice any such details. She couldn't quite put her finger on the fragrance. It was distinctive and warm, as if his presence filled the room. But of course, Vetiver by Guerlain.

An artist's sketch pad lay upon the cabinet. Ashton leafed through its pages, feeling like a naughty child, but hungry to know more about this man who moved her so, by studying the highly skilled freehand drawings. Bridges, faces, buildings — he wasn't just a remarkable architect, he was a wonderful artist!

There were so many facets to this man and so many things she didn't know about him. Funny that she should be sent on assignment to discover what she would have willingly researched of her own accord!

Still, if it hadn't been for the challenge of securing an article with this elusive man, she would probably be somewhere in the middle of a chilly European winter instead of in the land of Oz! Where would the yellow brick road lead her? Or was this just a short trip up the garden path?

Ashton was just leaving Karl's suite when the doors to the elevator whispered open. Stepping inside, she was greeted by the same waiter who had delivered her room service the day before. He began to grin from ear to ear. Oh great, thought Ashton, feebly attempting to rearrange her somewhat disheveled appearance. I bet I look like something the cat dragged in. He was still smiling to himself as Ashton gratefully escaped into the sanctuary of her own suite a few moments later.

Chapter Ten

After she had freshened up, Ashton turned her attention to Sam, her trusty laptop. His screen flickered to life as the familiar opening sound hummed from his built-in speakers. She had decided to start writing based on the few questions she had managed to ask. Her fingers sped nimbly over the keyboard as she composed the beginnings of what would become her feature article.

Karl Van Ness — she typed his name, savoring it. It was with some mirth that she recalled her father's warning to beware of this man and his reputation. Well, he had certainly surpassed all expectations! He was the first man to pique her interest in years.

Ashton reflected on the countless men she had been out with. Yes, she was the regular adventurer and the life of the party. She got on well with people and mixed easily, even in French! She had to, really, it was part of her job. But it had all been a facade, a screen to hide her pain and loneliness. She had never been serious about any of them, and had in fact never permitted any sort of emotional intimacy, not even with Brent. She may have walked away from that horrific crash, but she was not unscathed. A part of her had been scarred in a way that few could imagine.

Last night she had taken the first steps to letting go of the past. She hadn't expected it would be like this. She had wanted to deny her attraction to him, her yearning to be in his arms. She had imagined that if she ever met

"Don't you see, it is possible then. It could be him, just like in those spy stories . . ."

"Who could be him?"

"Never mind. I'm sorry I said anything." There was an awkward silence.

"Ashton, Ryan is dead. I'm sorry, but it's true. The sooner you accept it the better." He paused for a moment, unsure how to proceed. "What time is it there? It must be about 11:00 in the morning . . ."

"Yes. Why?'

"Why don't you go and get some sun? The fresh air will do you good. I think you've been working too hard. Quite frankly, I'm worried about you." He was almost having a conversation with himself. "Maybe I should come out there . . ."

"No!" Ashton took a breath, "I mean, I'm fine. There is no need to be concerned."

"I don't know, Ashton." He wasn't convinced.

"Brent, I'll be home in two weeks. Will you just relax."

"Okay, okay. But make sure you call me if you need anything."

"Sure. I'll talk to you soon."

"Okay, honey. Remember, I love you."

She couldn't make herself reply.

He's right, she thought as she hung up, maybe she just had a very overactive imagination. Well, at least she had convinced him that it was not necessary to get on a plane to Australia. She might have known he would react that way.

How was she going to pass the interminable hours till she would see Karl again? The anticipation was wonderful, delightful, torturous. Every minute that passed seemed more like an hour.

Ashton found herself fantasizing what he would be wearing when she saw him next. Who would speak first? How would she react? What would they talk about? Would he kiss her?

Ashton found it next to impossible to concentrate on anything work-related. Karl absorbed her thoughts. He affected the very blood that pulsed through her veins, the cells of her being. She didn't know whether to sit or stand, whether she was hungry or not. All she knew was that she wanted to see him, to be with him more than any other man she had ever met. Perhaps Brent was right. Maybe some sun would be a good idea. After all, she would be back in the winter of the northern hemisphere before she knew it. Swimming had always calmed her nerves.

She thought momentarily of the eccentric tarot card reader she had met once during a stroll through Balboa Park during a trip to San Diego. Ashton hadn't dabbled much in the occult, but found herself strangely drawn to the gypsy woman. Complete with black cape and purple tights, she had told Ashton that she was a fire sign, and that strange as it seemed, water would always be a source of comfort for her. At least she was right about that. She had also predicted that Ashton would fall in love with a man from her past.

Talk about clichés! Ashton had fully expected her to say that she would be taking a long journey too!

Who knew what she meant — a man from her past. After all, Brent had been in her past for as long as she could remember. Maybe that's who she had been referring to, though she couldn't imagine promising to love, honor, and obey him for the rest of her days. He just didn't spark that fire for her.

Ashton slipped into her bathing suit. Deciding that she was not in the mood to deal with the attention that this dangerous piece of attire usually attracted, she wrapped herself in a batik sarong and a linen shirt. Not a bad attempt at modesty, she mused, picking up her dark glasses and well-thumbed novel, before gliding out the door.

The sun was warm and comforting as Ashton stretched out lazily on a poolside deck chair. It was a hot day. From somewhere far below, the sounds of the city wafted up on the heat waves rising from the scorching asphalt. The sky was blue — a rich, intense slab of solid blue, reaching to the edges of space. High in the sky a solitary, thin wisp of a cloud hung. It was the pretense of a cloud, pretending to offer shelter, but somehow managing only to be decorative. Ashton didn't mind. She liked the heat, and was grateful for the opportunity to lie back soaking it in, her eyes closed to the world.

Ashton spent the rest of the day by the water, on the roof of a building overlooking a city. It didn't matter that it was a strange place to her, full of people bustling below, unaware of her looking down on them, racing like ants. It only mattered that she had the sun on her skin, and that she would see Karl tomorrow.

She was disturbed only by a waiter bringing her an order of fruit cocktail, and some club sandwiches. She tried to write in her journal, but her thoughts were too jumbled to write. She casually leafed through the pages of her half-read novel, only vaguely interested in the progression of the story. She discovered that she had read a whole chapter and had no idea what it was about.

Oh God, I can't be falling in love, can I? Though she didn't want to label it, to admit it, she knew that was exactly what was happening. She could focus on nothing except what it would be like to be in his arms once more. It was like being a schoolgirl all over again.

Chapter Eleven

A light breeze sprung up in the late afternoon, wafting in from the harbor. It caressed her skin now, dancing in the loose strands of her hair. The sun was beginning to drop into the horizon in the west, lighting the sky with a thousand shades of purple, red, and orange.

Ashton leaned casually against the brass railing of the balcony, watching the pleasure craft dotting the smooth waters of the harbor — tiny white dots on a smooth sheet of glass. There was even a tall ship returning to port, graceful and elegant, gliding effortlessly over the small white caps of the swells, a beautiful reminder of the country's colonial beginnings.

Gathering her belongings, she felt warm and relaxed, as she headed back to her suite. It had been a beautiful day, a much needed rest for her to gather her thoughts, and to try not to think about anything in particular.

She wondered for a moment if she should fire up the old adventurous spirit and explore some of Sydney's more interesting night spots. She'd heard some wild stories about The Cross and Oxford Street. But somehow after her peaceful day, she just couldn't muster the energy. Or was she perhaps being honest with herself for the first time in a long time?

Normally, she would have been off exploring, mixing with the locals, and experiencing the delights of a different culture. Not tonight however. "Well, Ashton Cameron," she thought, "it looks like it's the good old in-house video for you." Ordering the spicy chicken Caesar salad from the room service menu, Ashton retreated to the bathroom.

She had just stepped from the steaming shower, when she heard the rap at the door. *Now that's what I call service!* Scarcely taking the time to dry herself, she hurriedly wrapped her robe about her. She felt like she could eat a horse — wasn't it an eternity since lunch?

The precise, measured knock sounded again.

"Coming," she called. She stopped briefly to make certain her robe was fastened, since she was still dripping wet beneath it. *I wonder if it is my favorite waiter,* she thought, opening the door.

"Karl!"

"Hello, Ashton."

"Karl, what are you doing here?"

"Well, I'm glad to see you too!" He laughed.

"No, I mean . . . I thought you were away till tomorrow."

"I was supposed to be, but I had a wonderful incentive to gets things wrapped up quickly." He grinned.

Her heart pounding violently, Ashton stood gazing at his broad figure in the doorway. She was aware of her body beginning to tremble beneath her robe. She felt excited, vulnerable, embarrassed, shy, and so ecstatically happy. There wasn't a shred of her sophistication to be found anywhere . . . though she looked.

"You are going to invite me in, aren't you?"

"Oh . . . of course . . . I wasn't expecting . . ."

"Obviously not," he growled, encircling her waist and pulling her to his chest, before she had time to think.

He was close, so close that it seemed her heart was beating inside of his chest. Ashton was dying for the touch of his lips again, aching with expectancy. He bent his head to hers, his lips pausing a moment away from a kiss. With his free hand, Karl suddenly produced three envelopes, and chuckling, waved them in front of her nose.

"Choose," he said

"But, what is . . ."

"Choose," he said again, his voice more warm and resonant.

Ashton, delighted and frustrated all at the same time, wanted to kiss him so much. She couldn't stop laughing. "This one." She pointed to the smallest of the three envelopes fanned before her.

"Okay, Princess." He bowed gallantly. "Voilà! You have won dinner for two on the Harbour. Come on, let's go." He extended his arm.

The laughter and fun in his voice made her feel shy. Why, she didn't know. But it was a beautiful, warm feeling to be with someone so sexy and educated, yet who was filled with such a sense of . . . well, there was no other way to put it . . . fun.

"But Karl, now? I'm . . . I'm not even dressed.

"Well frankly, I prefer you this way. But if you insist, I will wait — impatiently — but I'll wait."

She could feel the hot waves rising. In spite of the plush robe, there seemed to be nothing protecting her from the appreciative intensity of his gaze. So excited she could barely think, Ashton flew to the closet and seized her favorite little black dress and patent heels. Her hands were shaking as she fumbled with the crossback straps on her dress, nearly fell when she was putting on her shoes, and managed to drop her pearl earrings twice.

She heard Karl laughing from the living room. He called to her, "Are you having a party in there without me? More importantly, do you need any help?"

"Oh hush. You're not helping matters at all." She couldn't stop giggling.

She finally sat down and began to put her hair up, still laughing, when all of a sudden she caught sight of a ravishing stranger in the mirror. Her face seemed not to be hers at all. She glowed with excitement. Her skin was luminous, her eyes shining with all the excitement of a little girl with a new toy. How she loved surprises! Ah yes, a rose would be . . . .

The husky warmth of Karl's voice stopped her, "Would my Lady like a rose for her hair?"

Their eyes met in the mirror and it seemed the very earth stopped for an instant. Without a word he stepped behind her and placed the coral rosebud in the curve of her French twist. He kissed her neck, so softly she almost wasn't sure he had. The tension between them was so thick it was tangible.

"Don't go away," he whispered in her ear.

Ashton couldn't have moved even if she had wanted to. She reminded herself that breathing was healthy, and permitted herself to exhale as he left the room. He moved like a big cat, powerful and yet graceful.

Karl returned an instant later, placing a white box tied with a coral ribbon, upon her dressing table.

"You might need this tonight. It could be chilly on the Harbour."

"Karl, how thoughtful of you. Thank you."

"Well, are you going to keep me in suspense? Go on, open it."

Ashton tore at the ribbon with delighted glee.

"Oh Karl, how beautiful . . . lt's perfect!"

Ashton caressed the folds of a silken black lace shawl nestled in the white tissue. His arms reached around her, and he lifted the gossamer fabric out of the box. She was aware of his warm body standing behind her. "Allow me," he said, placing it around her shoulders. He moved his hand from her shoulders to the curve of her cheek. In the mirror, she saw the look of desire in his eyes as he gently caressed her face. His voice husky, almost to himself, he whispered, "You're even more beautiful . . ."

Ashton thought she saw that same look of sadness in his eyes, the same look that she had noticed that first night on the balcony. It vanished so quickly, replaced by the radiant warmth of his smile, that she thought she had imagined it. "Karl . . .?"

". . . than last night, my Lady. You look ravishing. Shall we?"

Ashton accepted his proffered arm. She felt happy and light as Karl escorted her from the dressing room. She hadn't felt really happy in years.

As they opened the door they were greeted by an upraised fist about to knock. Oh no, it's my favorite waiter, again! Suddenly Ashton remembered the Caesar salad that she had ordered a century ago, or so it seemed.

"Well, good evening, Troy," Karl said smoothly, totally unruffled by the bemused expression on the waiter's face. "I'm afraid Ms. Cameron won't have time for that this evening. Please put it on my bill. Goodnight."

"Uh, yes, Mr. Van Ness, uh . . . goodnight. . . ." Troy was left alone, mouth agape, clutching his Caesar salad, as Karl and Ashton disappeared into the elevator.

The gleaming brass doors opened to reveal the opulent lobby and inside it, Ashton, happily leaning on Karl's arm. A pair of American tourists who had been impatiently waiting for the lift smiled in approval as Karl gestured gallantly towards the beckoning foyer, "My Lady." Ashton felt herself blush and lowered her eyes as she walked between the two, almost like a guard of honor.

Ashton felt as though they had been enjoying a mad, passionate love scene in the elevator, and yet they hadn't even touched one another. The energy between them was so intense it was tangible. There was not one person in the lobby that did not turn to stare at them as they walked across the polished floor. Trying desperately to cover her self-consciousness she turned to Karl and asked, "How did you do that?"

"Do what?"

Ashton looked up at the soaring lines of the pale marble walls, the roof seeming to disappear into itself.

"Do that." She gestured upwards. "How do you make walls not seem like walls? How is it that I know I'm in a confined space, feel no walls around me, and yet I feel protected? It's so beautiful, Karl. It moves me deeply and I can't explain it."

"Ashton, I've never heard anyone describe my work in quite that way. Thank you."

"It almost has the sacredness of a gothic cathedral, and yet it's distinctly modern, and functional."

"Come here, I want to show you something." He grabbed her and in his excitement practically dragged Ashton across the floor. "Look up there. You see that opening above the bank of elevators, that's open to the northeast and brings in the light that every artist dreams about. The other skylight over there captures the warmth and ruddiness of the southwest exposure and the setting sun. That's why my waterfall looks so different at different times of the day. In the morning, it's silvery blue with touches of gold. It always reflects the colors of the sky. Towards sunset, it's red and gold, like the lights in your hair, beautiful one."

He turned to face her, filled with excitement and eager to share the love of his work, and the tenderness he felt for her. Ashton was enraptured and delighted to see the exuberant child, practically dancing about in glee, within this powerful, strong man, normally so in control of his emotions.

He turned to face her, filled with excitement and eager to share the love of his work, and the tenderness he felt for her. Ashton was enraptured and delighted to see the exuberant child, practically dancing about in glee, within this powerful, strong man, normally so in control of his emotions.

"Karl, but where do you get the inspiration to create something so beautiful?"

He paused for a moment, eyes almost unreadable, as if looking into another world. When he spoke, it was softly, "Have you ever been trapped inside yourself, trapped inside your own body? it makes you want to soar beyond all human bounds and bonds."

Ashton looked into the handsome face of this bewildering, fascinating man. "Karl, how do you mean that?" She stroked his arm gently.

The soft vulnerability of the man disappeared in a flash, replaced in an instant by his customary dazzling charm. "Who knows what I mean? And where do you get your inspiration to write, Miss Cameron?"

"I don't know. I just do. From life, I suppose."

"Well then, why don't we talk about life over dinner."

"I'd like that. Where are we going?"

"That, my angel, is a surprise, and you will just have to come with me to find out."

"It appears I'm at your mercy." She smiled, surprised to find herself flirting. Yet it was real, it wasn't idle flirting, but something so intense — she didn't remember ever feeling so nervous, a giddiness in the pit of her stomach — that she had to treat it lightly.

His warm voice caressed his words, making her shiver in spite of herself, "It appears you are right." She felt his strong arm encircle her waist and they walked to their waiting car. Karl opened the door for her and said, "Just where are you going, my Lady? You're on top of the world now, remember? Or do you want to drive my Jag?"

"Oh!" Ashton blushed furiously and had to laugh at herself. "I could, you know, I'm an excellent driver."

"I know." He corrected himself quickly. "I mean, I'm sure you are." He smiled and gestured toward the passenger seat.

Chapter Twelve

Ashton slid into the deep bucket seat, sinking into the natural glove leather, inhaling the masculine scent of the car, and the unmistakable smell of Karl's Vetiver. Karl's eyes flashed appreciatively as he appraised the silken length of her long legs and the hint of lace at the top of her stockings. She was enormously relieved when he closed the door — that heavy "thunk" of quality — and prowled to the other side of the car.

Ashton marveled as Karl slid into the driver's seat, fired the engine to life and they were moving, all in one smooth motion, without apparent effort. She watched this exquisite animal at ease with his power, his grace, and his confidence. It was the sexiest flow of movement she had ever witnessed.

He wasn't trying to impress her; that was obvious. He seemed to accept the level of success he had attained, the quality of his life, and the power he commanded. The streetlights flashed and reflected themselves in the British racing green of the sleek machine. He downshifted for a stoplight and still they didn't speak, an almost meditative, comfortable silence growing between them, the tension of wanting to say . . . more like too much to say . . . stopping them.

He betrayed no trace of uneasiness shifting into first again with his left hand Ashton had never found it this easy to drive on the left side of the road She watched, almost mesmerized, as his strong hands masterfully controlled the gearshift, wondering what it would be like to be held in those arms, to be mastered by those capable, yet tender, hands.

Was this all some illusion? Neither of them had mentioned the other night, a fact for which Ashton was most grateful. She had resolved that it was his move now. She had never before asked any man to make love to her as she had last night, and it certainly wasn't going to happen again.

Lost in the magic of her reverie, Ashton didn't realize that the car had come to a stop. She had been intent on watching the smooth movements of his hands.

It was Karl who broke the silence first.

"Do you like the view?"

Ashton looked up to find them parked beside the water's edge, the water glimmering with the reflections of the city lights. Unwilling to depart from the place of quiet she was in, Ashton simply nodded. They sat quietly together. The only sound was that of the water slapping against the boardwalk.

Without looking at her, Karl reached over and gently took Ashton's hand, raising it to his lips. The caress was a whisper. Time had no meaning, the moment was endless, and suddenly he was on the other side of the car opening the door for her.

Snuggled by the water's edge, its warm lights beckoning, was the very chic restaurant, Le Lys Blanc.

The teak door swung open just as they approached, and Karl was greeted warmly by a pint-sized mustachioed man. "So wonderful to see you again, Mr. Van Ness. We have missed you." His beautiful accent made Ashton smile. It matched his perfectly dapper appearance, his slicked hair precisely parted in the center of his head, and his unmistakable French flair. She wondered if Karl knew all the waiters and restauranters in Sydney.

"Jean Marchand, may I present Miss Ashton Cameron."

The small Frenchman bowed ceremoniously, "You grace my restaurant, Mademoiselle Cameron."

"*Enchante de faire votre connaissance, Monsieur Marchand,*" Ashton replied in flawless French.

The little Frenchman puffed up like a peacock. "Ah! Not only incomparably beautiful, but incomparably intelligent. May I compliment you, Mr. Van Ness."

He strutted as he led the way to their table, nestled in a little nook flanked by palms, commanding a spectacular view of Sydney Harbour.

The warmth of the teak paneling, the place settings, the table linens, and the placement of a perfect Calla lily in a crystal vase was highlighted by a subtle downlight. Every detail breathed elegance. The White Lily — how perfectly named.

Even the crisp, white jacquard tablecloth had a barely perceptible pattern of a lily in its weave. The matching napkins were folded into the shape of a Calla lily, its stamen a tiny, delicate gold caviar spoon, placed inside the Baccarat crystal glass. All of the flatware was heavy, antique silver, a beautiful contrast to the simple lines of the silver charger resting inside the almost translucent English bone china.

Ashton's appreciation of her surroundings was interrupted by the arrival of a waiter, who, with a single deft flourish, unfurled the linen napkin and draped it across her lap. Almost at the same time, there miraculously appeared a beautiful silver tray with a mound of Beluga caviar set in a bowl of shaved ice. Half-buried in the snowy ice were two slender heavy crystal vodka glasses that were so cold they were frosty.

On the tray beneath the caviar were petite crystal bowls with chopped egg, the tiniest of Spanish capers, and finely minced onion. The bowls were separated by meticulously arranged toast points. The twin candles on the table made the whole scene shimmer with a magical warmth. In all her travels, Ashton had never seen any dish presented with such a quiet elegance and flair.

The waiter returned bearing a silver bowl containing, to Ashton's surprise, what appeared to be a block of ice. Karl grinned broadly watching the bemused expression on Ashton's face as the ritual unfolded before her. The waiter placed the bowl and its stand beside the table. He removed the white linen towel to reveal a bottle of Absolut vodka, frozen into the ice, from which he filled their two glasses, and promptly vanished.

"Karl, what an extraordinary place. I feel as though I've left reality, as if I'm in some fabulous dream world."

Raising his glass to hers, he whispered, "May all your dreams come true, Ashton."

Once again Ashton was silent, choked by the genuine emotions stirred in her by this man. She simply touched her glass to his, her eyes inordinately bright. She was so overwhelmed by the flood of emotions washing over her that Ashton could only gaze into the smiling warmth of the blue eyes opposite her.

Karl delicately scooped up a small spoonful of the caviar and leaned toward Ashton, "Try this, I think you'll like it." His voice was husky, intimate. He held the spoon close to her lips, and waited. She could feel all his desire contained in the simple gesture. Meeting his unwavering gaze, Ashton opened her mouth to accept the proffered delicacy. He held the spoon in her mouth for what seemed a moment longer than necessary, unwilling to break their physical contact.

She met his eyes as the hundreds of tiny eggs exploded between her tongue and palate. A taste so warm, delicate, and comforting like the sea, invaded her senses. She closed her eyes, swept away by the sensuousness of the experience. Then Karl's fingers were insistent on her mouth, gently guiding a tiny caper to the tip of her tongue. His hand tilted her chin up, and the chill of the crystal glass was against her lips, the icy liquor invading her mouth, mingling and complementing the subtle flavors. Karl lightly caressed the remaining drops of vodka from her lips. She opened her eyes to see him lick his fingers, and lean languorously back into his chair.

Ashton exhaled a shuddering breath. How on earth was she going to survive dinner and maintain her dignity, if every bite was like this? Struggling for composure, she murmured breathlessly, "Thank you, Karl. That was quite an experience."

"The pleasure was all mine, I assure you."

"No, it wasn't all yours." Her remark surprised them both. For all her propriety and fine upbringing, there was a delightful imp lurking within her just waiting for a moment of mischief. Her laughter rang out and caused more than a few heads to tum.

"Why, you little minx!"

"I gather you have a fondness for them?"

"For whom?" He raised an eyebrow quizzically. "Minxes, or whatever the plural of minx is? I think I'm developing one."

The return of the waiter to ask Karl what wine they wished to accompany their meal interrupted their banter. Casting his eye over the list, Karl selected the Chateau Latour '72. Ashton could hardly believe her ears. "But Karl, that's over 51 years old!"

"Oh, do you prefer something fresher?" He chuckled, "I can go pick some grapes if you like."

"I thought you only drank Dalwhinne anyway."

"It's your fault. You've compelled me to make an exception."

"Karl Van Ness, you're telling a fib and your nose is growing. I don't think there is anyone in the world who could compel you to do anything."

"Compel, perhaps you're right. Coax, cajole, convince — now that's different. Shall we discuss it, or should we save that for later?"

"Actually, I'd like to know more about you right now."

"What in particular? You have a captive audience. I hang suspended on your every word."

"Well, for instance, where did you grow up? Where did you study?"

"This sounds awfully like an interview to me. You know I don't give interviews."

"Oh, but I have permission," she quipped lightly.

"From whom?"

"Why, from the man himself — Mr. Karl Van Ness. You're acquainted with him, aren't you?" Ashton thought she saw his jaw twitch slightly and a veil shroud his eyes.

As she would realize later, there was an almost imperceptible pause before he replied, "Well yes, I made him."

Chapter Thirteen

The next three hours passed like lightening. It was a multileveled experience — a delightful dance of wit, sensuality, verbal barbs used most judiciously, excitement, and rapture. The food was a symphony of tastes. There was sorbet between each course to refresh the palate, Chateaubriand for two that melted in the mouth, a Bearnaise so light it floated, tiny baskets of pomme frites filled with exquisitely steamed vegetables, and red wine with a bouquet so full and round it defied description.

There wasn't a subject they didn't touch on, but there were gaps, and Ashton yearned to know more. He was the most real man she had ever known. He had a surety of self, but Ashton suspected that so much lay hidden beneath his polished exterior.

They were just starting on a beautiful dessert of crepes suzette, when the dapper French owner suddenly reappeared brandishing a glinting sword. Close behind him strode a waiter bearing two champagne flutes and an ice bucket, the top of the Moet et Chandon champagne bottle protruding over the silver rim.

Jean Marchand bowed formally and addressed Karl, "With your permission, Mr. Van Ness, some champagne for you and the lovely Mademoiselle Cameron, compliments of the house."

Karl nodded in assent. "Thank you, Monsieur Marchand."

Ashton watched wide-eyed as the little Frenchman drew the elegant saber from its scabbard, the fine steel glinting in the candlelight. He noted her amazement, explaining, "It is the sword of my great, great grandfather. He fought at the Battle of Waterloo."

The waiter handed the sword-brandishing Marchand the bottle of champagne wrapped in a fine linen towel, placed the glasses on the table, then stood well clear. The diminutive Frenchman held the bottle with his left hand extended slightly from his body and before Ashton knew what was happening, with a single deft flash of the blade, he cleanly sliced off the top of the bottle of champagne.

Ashton gasped in delight as the top of the bottle flew across the room, attracting quite some attention and smiles from the other diners. With a flourish, he turned to fill their glasses. "That Mademoiselle, is what we call, *sabre le champagne.*"

Ashton burst into delighted applause. "That is the most remarkable display I've ever seen. *Merci mille fois.*"

"My pleasure, Mademoiselle. Please enjoy." With that, he bowed politely and was gone. Ashton raised her glass. "Karl, here's to an exquisite evening. Every moment was a delight."

"Oh, but it's not over yet." Ashton didn't quite know how to take his last remark. He smiled at the look on her face, before continuing, "How about a moonlight stroll before your carriage turns into a pumpkin?"

She smiled shyly. "I'd like that a lot."

There was the faintest hint of a breeze coming off the water as Karl and Ashton sauntered casually along the boardwalk, hands loosely linked, their strides in perfect sync. Ripples of moonlight reflected in the undulating rhythm of the tide. The stars, so clear and so bright, seemed close enough to touch.

Ashton's shawl slipped from her shoulders, and they both stooped to catch it at the same instant. Karl replaced it around her shoulders and suddenly she was in his arms, her breath ragged and her heart beating so fast she couldn't breathe. All night they'd been wanting to hold each other like this. The anticipation had been the most delightful torture.

Karl's eyes were lit with a blue fire as his lips hovered above hers. The heat was coming off his body in waves. He began softly kissing the lobes of her ears, the hollow of her throat, and teasing her lips with his tongue but not actually kissing her.

Ashton thought she would go mad. A gasp escaped her parted lips as she thrust her fingers into his thick hair and pulled him even closer to her, the scent of him enveloping her.

She was aware of his hands exploring her body as they roamed over her shoulders, the small of her back, and the curve of her hips. Just when she thought she couldn't stand anymore, he kissed her. His mouth took hers in such an explosion of passion, that Ashton reeled with the waves of sensation that engulfed her. The ferocity of his kiss was almost painful, and then suddenly it became such a tender caress that it hurt even more. They broke apart, each visibly shaken to the core. It was Karl who recovered first, his breathing uneven.

"Cinderella, I believe your carriage is waiting."

Driving back to the hotel they again sat in silence, only this time it was a different kind of silence. Each of them was lost in their own thoughts — a distinct space between them. Ashton was filled with a nameless yearning. Was this love? Could she ever really love again, or was she merely trying to escape her deep loneliness?

Karl, in his own world, wondered why he felt no elation. His plan was working perfectly. Ashton was falling in love with him, and then he'd be able to walk out just the way she had left him. That's what he wanted, wasn't it?

Karl escorted Ashton to the door of her suite. She could feel him standing close behind her, his eyes watching her, as she fumbled in her bag for the key. She turned to face him as the door finally swung open. Karl was exercising every ounce of self-control he possessed, his eyes devouring her with wanting. His words came thickly, "I think I'd better go now."

Ashton's heart sank. She wanted to ask him to stay, to hold her again, to feel him close to her. Instead she heard herself saying, "Thank you again, Karl, for a beautiful evening."

He was about to turn to leave, when Ashton quickly blurted, "But when will I see you again?"

"That, my Lady, depends on you." With a deliberate flourish, he produced the two remaining envelopes from his breast pocket and said, rather seriously, "Go on, choose."

Chapter Fourteen

Ashton shut the door behind her, the envelope she had chosen clenched in her moist palm. How did he manage to have such an effect on her? What has he got that nobody else has ever had? Kicking her shoes off, she opened the doors to her balcony, and with a sigh of exasperation, sat heavily on the chaise. What an unbelievable night!

The little voice in her head had wanted to scream after him as she watched his broad back disappear down the long corridor. How could he just leave? How could he kiss her tonight the way he did, and just leave?

"Ashton," she kicked herself, "how could you have asked when you would see him again?"

She was up pacing now, furious with herself for blatantly showing her heart when she had resolved not to do it.

Looking up at the Southern Cross, the distinct stars glimmering against the dark night, she found some consolation in their peaceful radiance. After all, she was trying to leave the past behind. She was beginning to live again, and part of that living was asking for what she wanted, and having the courage to risk her heart.

And how did she know what tomorrow would bring? Tomorrow. Would she see Karl tomorrow? She gazed at the twisted envelope lying on the chaise. Slowly walking towards it, she speculated as to its contents. What on earth could he be planning next? Taking the crumpled paper in her hands once more, she smoothed its crinkles and carefully opened it. Removing a small card, she read in Karl's unmistakable script:

> Time: 10 AM
> Place: The Sea Witch
> Activity: Picnic for 2
> Sailing | Dress: Optional

Ashton stared at the card in her hand, dress optional — the sheer nerve of him. But he was taking her on a cruise! Her heart leapt with delight at the thought of being with him again, her doubts of a few moments ago swiftly vanishing.

She looked at her watch. It was nearly midnight. She had a whole ten hours to wait. How would she ever bear this long night ahead? Thoughts of Karl consumed her. She could think of nothing else.

She replayed in her head, for the thousandth time, the way he had slipped the caviar into her mouth. His smile illuminated her thoughts: the scent of him, his lips against hers, the taste of him — she had committed every detail to memory. How she would ever get any sleep tonight, she had no idea.

Karl slammed the door to his suite behind him. He stalked across the room, flinging his jacket on the couch, as he headed for the shower. He had not expected to feel like this. Why should he feel so torn? His plan was falling into place? Why did he want so much to be with her right now?

Seeing Ashton again had reopened his old wounds. He had wanted to teach her a lesson. But now this — to find her more beautiful and desirable than ever. His scheme was beginning to backfire badly! Every moment in her company tonight had delighted him. It had been as much as he was able to bear, waiting for an opportunity to kiss her. As he shed his clothes and plunged into an icy shower, Karl had no idea how he had managed to say goodnight a few moments ago and walk away.

Sitting on the edge of his bed, the large bath towel drawn loosely about his waist, Karl ran a tense hand through his damp hair. He sat deep in thought, weighing the pros and cons of disturbing Evelyn, before finally reaching for the phone.

Relieved to hear her silken voice when she finally answered, he spoke dryly, "It's me."

"Obviously Karl. Do you know what time it is? Are you all right?"

"I'm sorry I woke you," he paused, "Evelyn, I'm not sure if I can keep doing this."

"Keep doing what, darling?" Her voice was soothing and encouraging.

"Ashton."

"I see." Evelyn understood. She could feel the conflict in his tone, in the way he uttered that one word. "Karl, did something happen tonight that you want to tell me about?"

"No."

"Did she tell you anything about her past?"

"No. She has as many secrets in her closet as I do in mine. She was rather evasive about certain subjects – well, hell, so was I."

"She said nothing about Ryan?"

"No."

"So you find yourself falling in love with her all over again, but you're afraid to."

"Evelyn, you have the damnedest way of putting things."

"It's true isn't it?"

"I don't know if I want it to be. I don't know if I can take it again."

"Karl, dearest, you can only take one day at a time. But remember this, sooner or later you're going to have to confront your past with Ashton, whether you want to or not. You can never hide from the truth. You can run all you like, but sooner or later it always catches up with you."

"But I'm not Ryan Brooks anymore. Does that mean that all that I have achieved as Karl Van Ness is a lie?"

"Not at all. It just means that it is time to deal with this particular ghost and put it to rest. Karl, you don't think Ashton just happened to turn up in the same place, at the same time, at the other end of the world, for no reason at all, do you?"

He was silent for a moment before answering reluctantly, "I guess not."

"All right then. Now, why don't you try and get some rest? I know that this has all been very sudden, but I also know that everything is going to work out for the best."

"Evelyn, as always, thank you, and I'm awfully sorry I woke you up. I just needed to talk to somebody."

"That's all right honey, get some sleep."

Karl replaced the receiver gently. Pouring himself a spring water from the bar, he sat on the bed again thinking of all Evelyn had said. He looked at the spot where Ashton had lain, and thought of how he had held her, how he had undressed her and the fierce protectiveness he felt for her. Evelyn was right. Without hesitating a moment longer, he picked up the phone again and promptly dialed 1305.

Ashton answered almost immediately, "Hello."

"This is the Captain of the Sea Witch, calling to see if I have a crew for tomorrow."

"Karl!" Her surprise and delight was obvious. "How good to hear your voice . . ."

"I didn't wake you?"

"No. I was up."

"Well, do I have a crew for tomorrow or are you already booked?"

"I would love to go sailing with you tomorrow. You seemed to already have decided what I should wear! At least I won't have to worry about that," she laughed.

"Well, I'll leave that up to you. But I didn't think you would mind a suggestion."

"I'm sure the locals might raise an eyebrow or two."

"Oh, I don't know. You'd be surprised at how broadminded these Aussies can be."

"Karl, at the risk of sounding like a broken record, thank you again for tonight. I can't remember having enjoyed myself so much in a long time."

"I feel the same way, Ashton," he paused, fighting with himself, wanting to go to her right now. Finally he whispered softly, "Sweet dreams, angel. I'll see you in the morning."

Ashton had the most restless night of her life. The anticipation of seeing Karl again was the most excruciating and wondrous experience she had ever known. She slept fitfully for a few hours, and no matter how she tried, sleep evaded her until the first rays of the sun crept over the horizon.

Ten o'clock! Ashton was ready and waiting by 7:00 AM. She read, or attempted to, but the words didn't seem to make much sense. She polished her toenails with her favorite shade of antique coral.

The hands of the clock were moving like molasses. In sheer frustration, Ashton rang the front desk. "Hello Linda, yes, it's Ashton Cameron. My watch appears to have stopped, can you please give me the correct time? What's that? . . . 8:15 AM? Oh. Thanks a lot."

Chapter Fifteen

It was with great restraint that Ashton forced herself to walk slowly to the door when Karl's unmistakable knock sounded. She paused for a moment to throw on her favorite peach linen shirt and adjust her new bikini with its matching sarong. Opening the door, the look on Karl's face was just what she had hoped to see.

"Well, you certainly are shipshape this morning," he intoned, with the barest hint of a smile.

"Awaiting your orders, Captain." She saluted and winked.

"Insubordination!" Karl roared, seized her around the waist, and spun her around in a circle. "All right, what are we waiting for, let's go."

"Karl, wait a minute, my things . . ."

"You've got me, what more could you possibly need?" he answered, still not putting her down.

"Well, my sunscreen for one thing," she retorted. Hands pressed against his chest, she tried vainly to escape. "Karl, my bag is over there . . ."

Ashton was cut short in mid-sentence as he released her suddenly. She squared her shoulders, and stomped over to her bag in a pretend pique. Slinging the bag over her shoulders, and grabbing her sandals with the other hand, she sauntered past Karl with elaborate casualness without so much as a glance in his direction, and walked straight out the door.

"There are severe penalties for mutiny," he called after her. In two bounds he was beside her, and had playfully seized her braid. Undaunted, Ashton marched on, leaving Karl to hold her silk scarf in his hand. Reaching the elevator before he did, Ashton pressed the button and turned to watch him walk toward her. Lord, but he was a handsome man!

"What sort of penalties do you have in mind, Captain?" She looked at him innocently.

Karl, unable to bear it any longer, let out a deep growl. Lifting her clean off her feet he kissed her. It was brief, but there was no mistaking its intensity. Gazing at her with smoky eyes he said, "Do you have any idea what you're doing to me?"

Ashton wondered silently if he had any idea what he was doing to her.

Regaining his composure he added, "Come on, if we don't go now, we'll never get there."

The sky was cerulean blue. The day could not have been more perfect. Ashton watched Karl at the helm of the 30 ft. Sea Witch. Was there any place that this man was not at ease, she wondered?

She lay reclining lazily in the deck chair, the sun warming her, the spray glistening in the sunlight, misting her skin, as the Sea Witch cut through the gentle swells. Karl looked relaxed and happy as he navigated the vessel through the harbor. There wasn't a trace of the wariness she sometimes noticed in him.

He called to her, "Isn't this one of the most beautiful harbors? You know, they held the regatta here for the Olympics in 2000."

"My father ran extensive coverage of the event. I remember him saying the Australia Day Regatta on Sydney Harbor is the oldest continuously running annual sailing event in the world. I'd love to see that."

They were silent for a moment, enjoying the beauty of the environment around them. It was some time before Karl pointed to a small island they were passing. "See that? It's known as Pinch Gut. In the early days of the settlement here, convicts were often marooned there with only starvation rations."

Ashton looked at the island and thought about how harsh life must have been. "Karl how do you know so much about this place?"

He flashed her a broad smile from behind the helm, "I try to come here at least once a year. It's a refreshing place for the spirit and for the body. Australia is one of the world's best kept secrets. Do you know that I've even become intrigued by their unusual ritual and national sport of cricket? It's the only game you can play for five days and end up with a draw," he laughed. "If you're really lucky we can catch a game."

"No thanks. I don't even like American football."

"And just what kind of games do you like, Miss Cameron?"

"Solitaire."

"Solitaire? That seems most inappropriate for such a beautiful woman." Karl laughed. "I would have thought you were a fan of all contact sports."

Ashton thought she heard more than light banter in his tone and responded in kind "No, Karl, contrary to what everyone, and I mean everyone, seems to think, I have spent a lot of time alone. That is when I'm not up to my ears in my work, interviews, deadlines — but even then, when I write the articles I'm alone with Sam."

"Sam? Who is Sam?"

"Oh he and I have been together for quite a while. I don't think we could exist without each other," she continued lightly.

"I see.

Seeing the look on Karl's face made Ashton's heart fall, "Oh Karl, I'm sorry, I was just teasing you." Ashton was on her feet trying to see his eyes, hidden behind his sunglasses. "Yes, there is a Sam, but he's my laptop, he's gray and he's awfully square, but very reliable!"

Her hand, on his arm, felt his body relax and standing on tiptoe, she kissed his shoulder very gently. He kept one hand on the wheel and with the other he pulled her close to him. The tenderness at that moment was so intense that neither of them wanted to move or speak.

"Are you hungry?" he asked, still holding her close to him, "Perhaps something cool to drink?"

"Uh huh . . ." Ashton didn't move, "that would be nice."

"Well you're going have to detach yourself, my little octopus, and steer!"

"Aye, aye Captain."

Ashton was so quietly happy at this moment, the teak deck warm beneath her bare feet and the wind toying with her straw Panama hat. This land was truly remarkable — the light, the smells, the clean air — and certainly not least of all, this mysteriously familiar, yet totally unpredictable man that stirred her beyond all reason.

Ashton was just beginning to feel comfortable steering the big craft when Karl reappeared from below deck, bearing a drink in each hand. He handed her a tall glass filled with a beautiful concoction of crushed ice and thick mango juice. It was garnished with a flayed strawberry and a sprig of mint. Taking the wheel from her again, he pointed just up ahead, and said, "I know a lovely little spot just up here where we can drop anchor for a while. The swimming is great."

Ashton stood close to him, sipping her mango delight, its sweet, rich, thick texture sliding down her throat, watching as Karl guided them into a tiny, sheltered little cove.

"Karl, the flavor of these mangos is so different from the ones I've tasted in the Philippines."

"Yes, the pawpaws are too."

"The what?"

"Oh, I mean papaya. That's what they call them here." Ashton merely smiled.

The water was as smooth as glass and the breeze gentle, as they dropped anchor and Karl headed below, only to reappear a short time later with a picnic basket laden with exotic delights; cheeses, fruits, nuts, cold meats, pate, and fresh breads. Ashton hadn't realized how hungry she really was until Karl spread the banquet before her. They enjoyed a luxurious, lazy lunch, snacking, chatting, and laughing relaxed in the warm sun beating down on them.

Chapter Sixteen

Karl was sprawled full-length on one of the deck chairs, like a big cat basking in the sun. He turned to Ashton and asked almost sleepily, "So tell me about your travels. When did you first go to Europe?" Swallowing some Camembert, Ashton thought for a moment, "Oh, that must be at least ten years ago now, maybe even eleven. Why?"

"Just curious. Were you just being a tourist, or running away from home?"

"Actually my parents had arranged for me to go to a finishing school in Switzerland. They'd been wanting me to expand my horizons for quite some time."

"Sounds like you didn't really want to go."

"I didn't. I was young and very sheltered and the reason for staying home wasn't there anymore." Her face was sad. "When you're young, you think you know so much, your world is so secure, and then, as you get older, all you seem to find out is how much you don't know! It's a bit of a rude shock, really."

"I agree with you there." He paused for a moment, trying to read her from behind his dark glasses. "So you went to Switzerland, and that's where you learned to speak French?"

"Yes. And I traveled a lot, met interesting people, and decided that journalism was a career that really pulled me."

"I find it hard to believe that someone hasn't swept you off your feet yet. How is that, Ashton?" He sat up, and slowly removed his glasses, examining her with his intense gaze.

"I . . . I . . . just haven't met Mr. Right, I guess."

"Hasn't there been anyone special?"

Ashton sat thinking, wondering whether she really wanted to dredge all this up again. Finally she answered, "Yes, there was. It was a long time ago now."

"Well, what happened?" he asked gently.

A moment of pain flashed across her beautiful face, "Oh, just life . . . life got in the way."

Karl sat staring at her, the slightest hint of a frown creased his brow, as he wondered whether he should pursue this. Before he could speak, she continued, "You know, you remind me of him a little. I tried to tell you the other night when . . ." she paused slightly embarrassed, "It's your eyes. They remind me so much of someone I once knew. I never thought I would see eyes that blue again."

She was lost in a reverie, speaking almost to herself, "You know it's quite strange, but he was an excellent artist too."

The cry of a gull broke her chain of thought, and she looked at Karl tenderly, "I'm sorry, I don't mean to speak of the past. You were right, you know. I've spent too much time living with a ghost, but that's all over now."

"It's all right, Ashton, I asked you . . . How about a swim?"

"You go ahead, I think I may sink, I've eaten so much! I think I'm just going to lie here and catch some sun."

"Okay, but remember to put on some sunblock. The sun is stronger here than you realize." Ashton rummaged in her bag, producing a tube of Ultra Violette. "Would you mind?" she asked, handing him the tube. "Although I'm flexible, I can't quite reach the middle of my own back!"

"I'd be happy to."

Ashton removed her linen shirt, rolled over on the deck chair, and held her breath in anticipation of his touch. She could hear him squeezing some lotion onto his hands, then the sound of him warming it and rubbing his hands together. She caught her breath as the warmth of him touched her skin, massaging the lotion across her back. Ashton lost herself in the delightful simplicity of the gesture, and the sheer pleasure of feeling his hands gently caressing her body.

"Okay, Princess, that's it." He was wiping his hands. "Or is there more of you that needs some attention?"

"Mmmm, now that's a thought," she muttered sleepily.

"I'll see you very shortly." Ashton heard the splash and felt the boat rock slightly as Karl launched himself from the deck. She could hear him in the water as she dozed, basking in the warmth of the summer sun.

It was the perfect day. Ashton felt content and happy. She felt the sun warming and healing the sad, hurt places in her heart. She was reflecting on how good it was to be alive, as the boat shifted slightly with the weight of Karl pulling himself aboard again. He glanced briefly in her direction.

Ashton lay perfectly still, her sunglasses masking her eyes. She watched him as he grabbed a towel and started to wipe the rivulets running down his bronzed skin. He looked like a god to her, his body lean, hard, and athletic. Ashton gasped silently as she saw him run his fingers absent mindedly over his sternum. There again, was the long shadow of a scar. His legs too, for all their strength and muscular definition, were not unscathed. What on earth could have happened to him, she wondered?

He slipped on a shirt, and walked quietly to Ashton's side. She watched him watching her, the sunlight catching in the water droplets in his dark hair, still not giving any hint that she was awake. He sat softly beside her, and taking her feet in his hands, began to massage them gently.

"Mmmm, Karl, don't stop," she murmured.

"Well, hello sleeping beauty. Did you miss me?"

"Absolutely. How was the water?"

"A little on the cool side, but very refreshing"

"Karl, may I ask you something personal?"

His jaw twitched faintly, but he smiled and answered unconcernedly, "Of course, what is it?" "Karl, how did you get those scars on your body?"

"Do they bother you?"

"Oh no, they're hardly noticeable. I was just curious. I didn't mean to offend you. I'm sorry."

"It was a bad accident a couple of years ago. I'm lucky to be alive. Every day is a bonus. I don't like to talk about it. It was a very difficult time in my life."

"Oh."

They both sat silently, looking at each other, Karl wondering how much he could tell her. He wanted to tell her the truth, yet was trapped by the charade of his own concoction. Ashton sat wanting to fire a thousand questions in his direction. Thoughts of Ryan, his eyes, the car accident flashed through her mind, but she sat silently holding her tongue, fearful of driving Karl away and ruining their growing intimacy.

He stood up suddenly, and looking at the sky said, "Well, it's about 6:37, so I guess we better be heading back now."

"Karl!" Ashton was incredulous, "You're obviously a good sailor, but I've never heard anyone being so precise!"

"It's an old family secret," he said very solemnly, "Rolex." He held up his wrist and flashed the classic signature watch, laughing at the expression on her face. "Come on, and help me get these things below. It's time to sail off into the sunset with me."

As they weighed anchor and turned the boat back towards Circular Quay, Ashton's sense of closeness to Karl was deeply disturbed. The pull toward him was almost overwhelming. The whirling questions in her head, a wedge driving them apart. She had to ask him more questions. No matter who he was. Ashton knew she was falling head over heels in love.

"Karl?" she whispered as she nuzzled closer to him.

He was intent on navigating the narrow channel and

muttered absently, "Hmmm?"

"Who are you really?" Her voice was soft, the question guileless, but its point struck Karl like the point of a sword.

Eyes fixed straight ahead, he knew he couldn't lie to Ashton anymore. But what was he going to do?

Turning to Ashton, he knew he had to tell her. Her cheek was soft under his hand. His words were measured, hesitant, "Ashton . . . I'm . . ." The words stuck in his throat. "I'm a man who is falling in love with you."

Chapter Seventeen

"Kar. . . ." He bent his head and covered her mouth with his. Their lips, sun-warm, salty, silken, burned with the desire they felt for each other. All of her questions and doubts vanished into the beauty of this moment. The taste of him was heaven. He wanted more, as he drew her tongue into his mouth, tasting her, possessing her.

"Oh, Ashton, how I want you . . . wanted you from the very first moment I saw you," he whispered huskily.

"Karl, don't you know I'm falling for you, too?" She strained to press her body closer to his, eager for his hardness, his scent. She wanted to make love right now, on the teak decks, on the warm wood, she didn't care where. All she knew was that she wanted him to become part of her, to cover her with his strong body.

She could feel the length of him against her, the pulsing of his desire. He wound her hair around his hand and pulled her head back, his kisses burning a line of fire from her throat to the curve of her breasts. Her nipples ached for the touch of his hands, his lips, his teeth. Pushing her bathing suit strap down, he uncovered one full perfect breast. He captured the pert coral nipple between his fingers, and was just lowering his lips to taste her, when the boat veered starboard.

In an instant, Karl had the both hands on the wheel, correcting their course. "Whew, that was close! You see the effect that sirens have on unsuspecting sea captains?"

"Ah, I see," Ashton had both hands wrapped tightly around his waist, her breasts against his back, her breath warm in his ear. "So I'm a siren and it's all my fault?"

"Yep!"

"Well, Captain, how do you usually handle the mermaids you encounter?"

"I don't know, it's a new problem. I have never actually met one. Until now, they were merely the stuff of legend. However, I do think we ought to get the Sea Witch home safely, and then get us home. How about that?"

"How fast can this thing go?"

They both laughed.

Kicking the door to his suite closed behind them, Karl still held Aston to him, not letting her go for an instant. Their lips were locked together, their murmurings indistinct, as they clung to each other.

Holding her head between his hands, his tongue traced the outline on one shell-like ear. Ashton's pulse was racing. Their bodies intertwined, and Karl's hard thigh was between Aston's legs. Her peach shirt joined the golden sandals already on the floor. Karl's tongue again invaded her mouth and her head reeled.

In one quick motion he untied the top of her bikini and her breasts were bare against his chest. It was silk-on-silk, the most exquisite sensation Ashton had ever felt. Karl was burned to the core by the twin points of fire. One arm wrapped firmly around her waist, his dark head bent to bite the undersides of her breasts, to kiss the tender inside of her elbow, to kiss everything but her nipples, as her hands held his head to her trembling body.

The ripples of desire surged up from the soles of her feet. Her breath came in shuddering gasps. Now Karl's tongue began to tease the points of her willing breasts. He tortured her nipples in ever smaller circles, his thigh supporting her weight, and suddenly the shuddering wouldn't stop. Ashton was riding on waves of her own warm wetness, the core of her exploding in a shattering crescendo.

Ashton was aware of being lifted in Karl's strong arms as he carried her from the doorway to the inviting couch. He cradled her against his chest and rocked her gently until her trembling subsided. Ashton felt unable to move, a luxurious lassitude pervaded her body, and there was nowhere else in the world that she wanted to be. Karl tilted her face to meet his gaze, and asked softly, "Are you okay, beautiful one?"

Her eyes never leaving his, she nodded gravely, "Oh Karl, I didn't even know where I was. I felt like I'd floated off the earth."

"And what did you find when you were there?"

"A very beautiful place. One I've never seen before, and one I very much want to share with you."

They sat intertwined in each other's arms, surrounded by the scent of desire, and a hint of the sea still clinging to their bodies.

He kissed the tip of her nose, and covered her face with a hundred tiny kisses. Her tongue darted out and brushed his lips as he continued to nuzzle her.

"Oh Karl, you taste like the sea."

"Hmmm . . . and you, young lady, taste like sunblock. How about a bath?"

"Yes, what a perfect idea." Karl caught her as she attempted to get up and her knees buckled. "You stay right here."

He returned with two champagne flutes and a perfectly chilled bottle of Dom Perignon.

"Had I have known you were coming," he paused significantly, "I would have had Clicquot on hand," he chuckled wickedly.

Ashton could feel herself blush to the roots of her hair.

The cork whispered off at his expert touch, and the two glasses were instantly filled to overflowing. Gently raising her head, Karl held the flute to her lips, caressing her tongue with the bubbles. Her mouth still wet with champagne, he bent and kissed her. "Here, darling, drink this." Kissing her again, he whispered huskily, "I'll be back in a heartbeat. I'm going to run a bath for us."

Ashton couldn't move. Her whole body had come suddenly and magically alive again, and yet she couldn't say again — she had never felt like this before. The soles of her feet tingled, her loins ached with a honeyed lethargy, her breasts felt burned by a sweet fire, and her lips were indelibly imprinted with Karl's kisses. She snuggled into the silken cushions and felt the surprise of her wetness on her inner thighs. This was being alive! Nothing else mattered except the touch of his hands, the scent of his skin, the way his deep, husky voice got inside of her and turned her insides to jelly.

How had any of this happened? Connecticut was thousands of miles away, not only literally. It was lifetimes away. Was it really less than a week ago that she had crossed the ballroom floor of the Osprey Hotel and been pulled to the man across the room? She heard Karl filling the tub. The champagne was cold and the bubbles tickled her nose. Ashton smiled at herself, how strange it was to feel so safe and protected, cared for? She really hadn't allowed that for a very long time.

Karl's voice beside her ear was soft, intimate, "And is my mermaid ready for her bath."

"Oh Karl," her arms went around his neck and suddenly she felt shy, her breasts bare to his gaze. Her arms crossed instinctively to shield herself from the bold eyes looking into hers. In one motion, he retrieved her shirt from the floor and covered her with it.

"Darling, no one would ever guess that you are shy. Don't be embarrassed by that. I think it's beautiful. But I think too, that you are a brazen hussy. You just don't know it yet!" His voice was soothing.

"And just how do you know that, Mr. Expert?" Ashton tried her bravado on for size — it didn't fit!

"You don't have to prove to me how strong and world-wise you are, Ashton. You are strong and you do know the world. But there is an untouched innocence inside of you, in spite of all your sophistication, that breaks my heart. It made me want to put my arms around you from the first instant I saw you. That's not a bad thing, Ashton, it's very rare and very beautiful."

Ashton felt her lips trembling, no one had ever seen into her soul this way. She didn't know where to hide, but then, she didn't want to hide either. She wanted to discover all of herself. Karl's arms enfolded her and the only sound was the comforting rhythm of his heart. She felt her breathing change, the fear of truly revealing herself begin to melt, and the sudden rush of desire flood her again.

Ashton's fingers entwined themselves in Karl's hair as he lifted her easily from the couch and carried her into the bathroom. Her legs were unsteady, and it seemed her eyes locked with Karl's were her only support. He gently took her shirt out of her hands and knelt to remove her bikini bottom.

Ashton felt her whole body quiver with wanting him. His hands slid up from her ankles to the tender skin at the back of her knees. His breath was warm on the moist center of her. His finger slid between her thighs and Ashton clutched at Karl's shoulders. He teased her tender lips, open, swollen with desire.

"Wet, hot silk, my darling — and all for me." Karl held her eyes with his as he raised his wet fingers to his lips. "Nectar from the sea, and from my very own mermaid — for me. Do you want me, Ashton? Do you want me as much as I want you?"

Ashton felt incapable of words, her heart was caught at the base of her throat. Karl cupped a handful of water and poured it over her breasts. It took her breath away.

"How is the water? Just right?"

Karl held out his hands to her from inside the deep, sunken tub. She stepped into his arms and slid into the warm, scented water. This tub was huge, much larger than the one in her suite.

The dark green Italian marble was the perfect setting for Ashton's strawberry and auburn hair and fair skin. "God, did she have any idea of how beautiful she was?" Karl wondered.

"This feels wonderful!" Ashton sighed luxuriously and turned on her back to float in Karl's arms.

"No . . . not yet. Stand up, you need to be washed. I don't want anything between us, not even sunblock," he chuckled.

He took a natural sponge from the side of the tub and began to wash her back with long, firm strokes. He lifted her arms as though she were a little girl and washed her breasts and shoulders, the warm water running over her like a caress. His desire for her throbbed between them and Ashton was mesmerized by the thought of him inside of her softness. He stroked her thighs with the sponge and moved down to her feet.

"Sit," he commanded.

"I will not," she retorted.

"Oh no?" He reached up for one coral nipple and playfully captured it in his fingers. Sliding his body up against her own, his other hand entangled itself in the triangle of curls between her legs and suddenly Ashton felt his hardness between her thighs. He moved only slightly, but the rubbing of his heat against her sensitive core was excruciating. His hands moved from her nipples to the small of her back and pressed her closer to him. His fingers slid down to the ripe cheeks of her bottom and began to spread them apart. Aston squirmed against him, consumed by desire, fear, curiosity and all her squirming only increased the delicious friction between her legs.

"Karl, you're torturing me. . . ."

"I certainly hope so, my darling."

His finger pressed insistently against the tiny, delicate opening of her bottom, driving her wild. All the while, he hadn't stopped kissing her.

"I'm going to kiss you everywhere; do you know that? And I mean, everywhere." His intensity, his insistent hardness, the controlled violence of his passion was too much for Ashton.

Chapter Eighteen

She pulled away from Karl and sat shakily on the edge of the tub. Instantly, he was beside her, concern written all over his handsome face. "Honey, I didn't mean to scare you. Look at me . . . I would never do anything to hurt you. I only want to pleasure you."

"Oh Karl, it isn't that I'm afraid you're going to hurt me," her voice was small, filled with wonder. "It's that I'm afraid I won't be able to stand all the sensations and emotions that you arouse in me. It's more than a physical reaction. It's as though I have been locked in a safe for a long time. This animal part of me — no, not a long time but always — has been chained up inside of me.

Karl sat at her feet in the tub, his arms resting on her knees gazing up at her with solemn eyes. "Tell me more, angel, I'm listening."

"The way you touch me, the way you want me, calls to something deep and primordial in my soul and it makes me want to burst out of that fireproof safe with a violence of emotion that scares me. I want to scream. It just feels as though if it all happens without first opening up the door of my self-made cage, I'll explode and cease to be. Does that make any sense to you at all?" Her hands held his head gently, her eyes smoky and bewildered.

"Yes, I know just what it feels like to be trapped inside of yourself. Yes, it is a shocking and shattering experience to suddenly meet the you who was trapped inside. Forgive me darling, I have wanted you for so long, that I forget we have not . . ."

"What do you mean? It hasn't been that long!"

"Yes, it has been hours since we've eaten. I'm famished!" Karl sprang to his feet splashing water everywhere and turned on the hand shower. "Would my Lady care to be rinsed and dried, although I think the latter is quite a hopeless task."

They laughed, but now the laughter was softer, more intimate. The rinsing, the elaborate drying was all part of their lovemaking.

Karl wrapped a towel around his waist and bowed to Ashton. "I'm attired for dining, are you ready?"

Ashton's eyes dropped to his makeshift sarong and she was convulsed with laughter.

"Are we going to eat in the tent or outside under the stars?"

"Why you little minx. . . ."

And in a flash he was after her, this beautiful, naked, erect satyr, bounding after her, brandishing a towel. Ashton was squealing with delight and vainly trying to elude him. She was nearly doubled over with laughter and could barely run. In an attempt to leap across the bed, she fell into the mounds of pillows, but quickly recovered and began hurling pillows at him with all her might, still unable to stop laughing.

Suddenly Karl was on top of her, pinning her wrists to the bed, his eyes at first filled with mirth, boring into hers with a probing intensity. Ashton felt her body changing, transforming itself, opening, pulsing.

"Karl, Karl . . . Karl, I want you. I want you inside of

me. I need you inside of me."

Karl began kissing her arms and slid his burning lips to her aching breasts. Her nipples were rigid points of pure sensation. He nibbled at the tiny tips, still holding her wrists with his other hand.

Ashton's hips thrust against Karl. "Oh Karl, now . . . now, I want you."

"Not so fast, my darling. Are you sure you want me? How much do you want me?" His fingers traced delicate patterns down over Ashton's stomach and slid to the hollow of her hip where he lingered, driving her mad

"Do you want me here? Right here?" His fingers invaded the throbbing core of her, and caressed the delicate, wet lips. He teased the tiny opening until Ashton thought she would die of anticipation.

"Oh, but my baby is dripping with honey for me . . .." Karl moved his thumb to the little hard button of her pleasure and began to invade her with his index finger. His touch electrified her. She found herself opening her legs wider, welcoming these delicious sensations.

She began to feel the deep trembling inside that she craved. It was only then that Karl moved to cover her body with his own, and she felt the head of his maleness at the tiny, hungry mouth between her legs. He stopped moving and it seemed the very earth did, too.

His eyes were all that existed. "Ashton, I love you."

Ashton could feel the throbbing of her own heartbeat at the moist core of herself. Karl inched into her tightness with agonizing slowness, her wetness easing the way. He began to move gently, deeply, and then in a mounting frenzy that enveloped them both. Ashton thrust back at him in ecstasy — the waves of her passion breaking over her in joyous profusion. Her back arched to meet his strength and Karl's cry echoed in the room. "Ash, oh Ash — I needed you. . . ."

The bright light of the full moon filtered through the open window, bathing the room in a magical glow. Entwined in each other's arms, Karl gently stroked Ashton's hair, and traced the outline of her full mouth with tender fingers.

They were wrapped in the intimacy of two souls having shared a timeless moment. In the quiet that surrounded them, Ashton had never felt closer to anyone. She kissed him gently on the cheek. Karl had awakened in her a yearning to be known, to be loved. She felt free, and safe to reveal herself in a way that had never before been possible.

Emboldened, she softly ran a finger over one of his nipples, playing with it, enjoying its softness beneath her touch. She traced a path over the hard muscles of his chest, slowly working her way down the line of hair till her hand slipped beneath the sheet. He watched through half-closed eyes at the delight and boldness on her face as she began to explore his body.

Aston watched with pleasure the effect she was having on him, as she felt his body tensing as her hand lightly made its way closer to the source of him. Karl groaned with pleasure as her hand encircled the width of him, caressing him, as if measuring him for size. Her eyes filled with delight as she teased him, stroking him, feeling his desire for her rise again. A surprised cry escaped her lips as he growled her name, "Oh Ashton." In one deft motion his body was on top of hers again, her legs spread wide to receive him. She gasped in rapture as she felt him unite with her, moving inside of her, and shuddered in ecstasy as he took her again.

Brilliant sunlight flooded the room. Ashton opened her heavy eyelids with considerable effort. Her body was washed with delicious exhaustion. She felt the weight of Karl's protective arm across her chest. He looked so peaceful right now, sleeping the sleep of one who was satiated. A smile of pleasure lit her face as she recalled their long night of lovemaking. A lifetime wouldn't be enough to explore all of life's delights with this man! Nothing could have prepared her for the way he took her that first time. Her fleeting experiences with Ryan all those years ago had been very awkward . . . a memory stirred.

What was it Karl had said to her last night? Had he called her Ash in the midst of their lovemaking? No, surely not. She must have imagined it.

She had been too overwhelmed by the sensations bombarding her to pay attention at the time . . . but . . . he had never called her that before. In fact, no one ever had, except — Ryan. She looked at Karl's sleeping form beside her, his handsome face so peaceful.

Was she completely out of her mind?

But the fact was, the more she found out about him, the more similarities there were to Ryan.

Showering his face with soft kisses, she smiled as he stirred, slowly opening his lids to gaze at her with his brilliant blue eyes. "Good morning, darling," she whispered, kissing him lightly.

He grinned. "Awakened by an angel. I could get used to this. Did you sleep well?"

"Never better, though for some reason, I feel awfully worn out this morning."

"Hmmm," he chuckled, "You're obviously not getting enough rest. You may have to spend the entire day in bed."

"Oh, do you really think so?"

"Absolutely!" They both laughed. "Are you hungry? How about some coffee?"

"Sounds great. I'm ravenous."

He lay there smiling at her. "I know!"

She slapped him playfully. "Why don't you stop casting aspersions on my fine character, and go and get us the room service menu."

"Okay, okay." Karl reluctantly slipped out from beneath the snug covers. Ashton lay quietly, watching appreciatively at the easy grace of his beautiful masculine body, as he walked over to pick up his robe thrown carelessly over a chair. He paused, grinning devilishly at her staring at him in all his naked glory, before slipping into his terry bathrobe. "You wouldn't want me to catch cold would you?"

Ashton picked up a pillow and flung it in his direction. He ducked playfully and was just turning to search for the menu when she called out to him, "Ryan, would you . . ."

She caught herself, not knowing where the words had come from. Without a moment's hesitation he turned to answer her. He stopped dead in his tracks, horrified at his slip, and at the look of disbelief on Ashton's face. Neither of them spoke. They stared at each other across the growing distance that separated them in that single moment.

Ashton sat staring at Karl, incredulous, not wanting to believe what she knew was true. Her gray-green eyes blazed with a fiery indignation as his gaze met hers.

"It is you, isn't it?" she whispered hoarsely. "How could you?

Karl stood expressionless, face void of emotion. "I could ask you the same question," he said coldly.

"What do you mean? Why didn't you tell me the truth? How could you! How could you continue with this cruel charade? How could you lie to me? How could you make love to me?" She shook her head in disbelief. "I can't believe this is happening!"

Karl was silent, his face implacable, fighting the urge to scream that he had tried to tell her.

"Karl, how could you, knowing how much I loved you?"

"Loved me? You loved me enough to leave me for dead," he said bitterly.

"That's not true."

"Oh no, then where were you?"

"They told me you were dead!" Ashton hurled the words at him.

"For God's sake, Ashton, do you take me for a fool?" he said harshly.

"It's the truth!" She felt tears rising to the surface, tears of relief, of anger, of hurt, all mixed into one.

"It's your version of the truth. You couldn't leave soon enough, could you? You could have at least had the decency to say goodbye."

Ashton sat sobbing silently, tears washing her beautiful face. He stood like stone, watching her, closing his heart to her grief. Time passed slowly. It was some moments before she finally regained her composure and looked at him again.

She felt like someone had driven a stake through her heart.

She spoke in shock, quietly, almost automatically, "Ryan did die in that accident. He never would have treated me the way you have. I love you. I loved you as Ryan, and worse for me, I love the man you are now, Karl. It doesn't really matter whether you believe me or not. My heart knows the truth. Someday you'll know it, too."

Without another word, Ashton rose to her feet, dressed in interminable silence, and walked towards the door.

"Wait."

She turned to look at him. She wanted to run to him, to fling herself into his arms, to scream that they shouldn't waste a minute of their time together, that it was a miracle to have found each other . . .but she didn't.

He opened the bedside drawer and retrieved something. He tossed it in her direction, "I believe this is yours."

Ashton looked down at the little band of gold with a tiny sparkle of light lying at her feet. It was the ring he had given her when he had asked her to marry him. She lost it in the car accident. As she looked at him, she thought of all the possibilities, of what might have been.

"Goodbye, Karl," she said softly, turned and left.

Chapter Nineteen

Closing the door to her suite, Ashton exploded into a flood of tears. How could he? There were no words to describe the anger and hurt she felt right now, strangely mingled with the relief of the miracle that he was alive.

She sobbed freely, venting the torrent of pent up emotions that she couldn't find words to express. Her heart was broken. Throwing herself on the bed, she cried an ocean, until there were no more tears left to cry.

When Ashton finally sat up and looked at herself in the mirror, the image that greeted her was surprising. Yes, she had tear-stained cheeks and swollen eyes. But there was also a calm in her face that had never been there before in all her 29 years.

Her torrent of tears had freed her and purged something from her being. She cared enough for herself to walk away from all she loved. Karl couldn't, or wouldn't, believe her. That astonished her. Perhaps for the first time in her life, Ashton discovered her own self-worth. That had nothing to do with her life of privilege. It was her integrity, something that money couldn't buy, that shone on her face now.

Karl, I love you. I have always loved you. I will love you until the day I leave this earth. Someday you will know the value of that. If all you believe is that I callously left you to die, then you don't really know me at all, and you don't deserve me. Ashton wiped the tears from her face, and gathered her composure.

I suppose I should tell Dad that it will take some time

before I finish that interview. I have a lot to say to my parents. They need to know how wrong they were and how their protectiveness almost ruined my life.

Ashton was just about to pick up Sam, when she noticed the envelope stuffed under the door. She had probably walked right over it in her hysterical state. She groaned as she read the fax from Brent.

"Ashton I'm worried about you. I'm catching a flight from JFK tonight arriving in Sydney Thursday morning see you then. Love Brent" The fax was dated 2 days ago.

I don't suppose I'm going to wake up in a moment and discover this has all been a really bad dream thought Ashton, looking at her watch. She realized he would be arriving within the hour. Well, at least she would have an answer to give him.

Forty minutes later she was an absolute vision of loveliness as she opened the door to find Brent's boyish face grinning at her. It was a comfort to see those familiar blonde locks swept back off of his face and his kind hazel eyes smiling at her.

"Surprise!"

"Brent, it's so good to see you."

"I thought you might miss this, so here it is!" He thrust an "I Love New York" bag at her and stood watching her expectantly. Grateful for the diversion, Ashton eagerly looked inside. She broke into laughter as she pulled a tiny, bright mint green, plastic model of the Empire State Building from the crumpled bag.

I just want you to know I scoured the airport's finest

boutiques for this exquisite gift."

"Brent, it's fabulous." She was smiling broadly. "I'm glad you're here."

He wrapped his arms around her, squeezing her in an affectionate bear hug. "Do you really mean that?" he looked deeply into her eyes and knew that she had been crying.

"Of course, I do."

I wasn't sure. I mean, I wasn't sure if you'd want to see me. That's why I didn't text you. I thought you'd tell me not to come. But Ashton, I had to come. I've been so worried about you."

"Brent, it's OK, I'm glad you're here. We need to talk."

"That sounds serious."

"No, just long overdue. Why don't we get some drinks sent up? You look a little tired."

"Sounds good to me. It really was an awfully long flight. Do you suppose they have to work really hard to get the food to taste like plastic, or does it just turn out that way?"

Ashton could only laugh.

"Ashton, I don't know how you managed to travel so much and still look as fabulous as you do. I feel like a wet rag right now!"

"Well, you look just fine to me."

"Ashton, it's so good to see you. I've missed you." He stepped closer to her, gently holding her by the shoulders.

He moved to kiss her, but Ashton raised her hand to

his chest, halting him in his tracks.

Shaking her head sadly, she said, "Brent, I can't."

"But Ashton, I love you."

Ashton brushed her hand wearily over her face. This was going to be more difficult than she thought. She led the way to the couch. "Why don't we sit down?

Waiting until he was seated, she continued, "Brent, it's no use. I can't pretend to love you in the way you want me to."

"Ashton, we've talked about this. You don't have to give me an answer now. Take all the time you need. I'll wait."

"Brent, I've made up my mind. I can't marry you."

He sat staring at her blankly. He couldn't understand what she was saying.

Incredulous, he asked, "But, don't you love me?"

"Yes, Brent, I love you. But not in the way that you deserve to be loved. I couldn't make you happy, because my heart would never be truly yours. You deserve someone who will appreciate you for everything you are."

She watched as he sat, head in hands, and waited for him to speak. When he finally looked at her his voice was toneless.

"There's somebody else, isn't there? The guy who's been sending you the flowers and taking you to the opera?"

"Yes."

Emotionless, he continued, "What's his name?"

Ashton couldn't bear to continue this torture. She

knew it was best to make a clean break of it and for Brent to know the truth."

"Karl Van Ness."

"The architect? The playboy?"

Ashton nodded.

"How long have you been seeing him?"

"Less than a week. But he's . . . "

He interrupted before she could finish.

"Ashton, you'll get over it. This can't be serious, it's just a summer fling — you don't even know the guy. Come on honey, let's put it behind us."

Ashton rose and walked to the window. She stood with her back to him, gazing at the Harbour for a few moments. This time the spectacular view offered no comfort.

Brent sat watching her. What a beautiful woman she had become. Oblivious to the breeze playing in her hair; her hands remained plunged in the deep pockets of her linen jacket. The slenderness of her silhouette made him ache with how vulnerable she really was, despite her remarkable strength.

He rose to join her, gently placing his hands on her shoulders. Turning her to him, he saw her eyes brimming with tears, threatening to overflow.

"It's serious, isn't it?"

A huge tear rolled down her right cheek.

"Oh, Brent. I'm so sorry. I wish I could love you as you deserve. You've been so good to me. I thought the feeling would change. But I just don't think I can love you as a wife should. I'm sorry."

He held her as the tears quietly trickled down her face.

"Ashton, I won't pretend I'm not hurt, but I want you to be happy."

"If this Karl, whatever his name is. . . ."

"Brent, there's more."

With a quizzical look, he stood waiting for her explanation.

"Ryan wasn't killed in that car accident." Her words hung suspended in the silence between them.

"Ashton, you know that isn't . . ."

She placed her fingers gently on his lips, and said, "Please, let me try and explain."

"No. That's enough. I've heard all I want to hear about this. Your head knows darn well that he's dead, and your heart just won't give up, will it?"

"But Brent . . ." She was surprised at the vehemence of his response.

"Ashton, I've watched you torment yourself for ten years."

He was pacing the room now.

"I've seen you close everything and everybody out of your life and bury yourself in your work. I've seen you virtually stop living. You are alive, honey. And I love you. Give me a chance. No, give yourself a chance. When are you going to understand that he's gone? You've got to go on with your life."

"Brent, I know this sounds crazy. I didn't believe it at first either, but Ryan is alive. Ryan Brooks and Karl Van

Ness are one and the same man."

She waited for him to reply. He stood, looking at her silently. She saw in his eyes the effort to understand, to comprehend for her sake. But she saw too, the hurt that her words had caused.

"Ashton honey, I don't think you understand. You see, ever since we were little kids, I've loved you. Everything I've ever done in my life was with the knowledge that you were a part of that life. Every plan I've ever made, every thought I've ever had for the future, was with the thought of you beside me."

"But Brent, I never made you any promises. I never once misled you or was anything but honest with you."

"But don't you see how perfect we are together, how perfect we've always been?"

The pleading look on his face almost broke her heart.

She steeled herself to continue, "Brent, how can you say that? Don't you remember when Ryan came into my life, how my entire world changed?"

"So you went crazy for a little while, that's all."

"No, Brent." She was solemn, her words measured. "I didn't go crazy for a little while. I found the love of my life. I found the man with whom I wanted to spend the rest of my days. I had found my mate."

"So you're going to marry him now?"

"No." Her voice was dull and heavy. "No, I'm not going to marry him."

"Now, I really don't understand. Why are we having this conversation if you're not going to marry him? Then everything between us is fine."

"Brent." She sighed. "I don't think I even know how to explain this to myself. But no, everything is not fine between us. I'm not the little girl that you fell in love with so many years ago. Ryan has changed too. The simplicity of the love we shared is not available to us right now. It's buried under anger, resentment, misunderstanding, and the passage of more years than I care to remember. Karl not only rebuilt his body, his face, and his world, but he walled up his heart even from himself. He is convinced I walked out on him knowing he was alive."

"Oh, but Ashton, that's not true."

"Brent, I can't convince him of that. We can only imagine what kind of agony he's been through."

"Ashton, if you can't get inside of those walls, nobody can. Why can't you give us a chance?"

"I can't do that, Brent. Don't you see that our life together would be a lie? I love you, but I love you like a brother. You're a member of my family. You're one of the dearest people in my life. I couldn't have survived without you. But no matter how I'd like it to be different, I don't love you the way I have always loved Ryan and will always love Karl."

"What are you going to do?" His voice was soft with concern.

"I don't really know. No matter how much I love Karl, no one can command a heart. It has to be his choice. Not all the love that I feel in my being can scale those walls unless Karl Van Ness allows it. You see, Brent, I don't just love him, I respect him. And you know something, more than that, I respect myself. I have a lot of love in this heart of mine, and passion, and fire, and I want the same out of my partner. You can't make anybody feel that. No matter how strong you are, you can't command a human heart."

Ashton was almost talking to herself, looking out at the calm waters of the Harbour.

"Brent, I want all of his love, all of his respect, for all of my life. If not, I prefer to be alone. There never will be, and there never has been, another man for me."

Ashton ran out of words. There was a stillness in her heart, and her voice was toneless. There was no drama, only truth.

"Ashton, I'm sorry."

She smiled at him, "So am I."

They stood looking at each other for a moment, before he continued quietly, "Are you hungry?"

"A little."

"How about me taking you for an early lunch?"

"Brent . . ."

"No strings attached." He raised his hands in surrender. "I think you could use a friend right now."

"Yeah, I reckon I could."

He gestured with his head towards the door. "Come on."

Their eyes met, and he looked at her with a face filled with a sad softness. He bent and kissed her tenderly on the forehead.

"You're quite a lady, Miss Ashton Cameron."

Chapter Twenty

Karl stood staring at the ring. He felt only a strange numbness and a hollow in his heart. What an empty victory. Was this really what you wanted, you damned fool? He raised his eyes to the door where Ashton had disappeared only moments before. She had walked out of his life for the second time, and with amazing dignity. He had wanted to run after her, to take her in his arms, to tell her that the past didn't matter anymore, but he made himself stop. His pride made him stop. He choked on the words he wanted to say.

Could she really have believed that he had been killed? Wasn't that just a bit too farfetched? Ashton was intelligent. Why wouldn't she have checked? She was a journalist for goodness sake! You don't just walk away without more information. Why did she believe her parents? But then, why wouldn't she believe them?

Karl, stop driving yourself mad. Haven't you relived those years enough? Haven't you wallowed in that pain more times than you need to remember? If you believe now that she never knew, that she really thought you dead, how can you justify all these years without her, having closed your mind to her existence? The agony of losing her was almost worse than the pain of the physical injuries that he had endured.

Why did he feel so sick? He stooped to pick up the ring where he had flung it on the carpet. The tiny glimmer of the gold ring recalled a time more innocent and simple, before the world had invaded their lives, before destiny had changed their paths. It was their beginning together, hopes and dreams awaiting their fulfillment. A love so strong and powerful, they naively thought that nothing could ever come between them. How young they were!

Smiling faces flashed through his mind, images of the women he had known, flirted with, spent time with. Time, measured by a clock. Hours of pretending devoted attention, vacuous laughter, fine champagne, exquisitely cut dinner jackets, perfumed hands.

What did any of it mean? Time. Any second that he spent away from Ashton — that was time. It weighed heavily on his heart, his mind. None of them mattered. All of those women were attempts to forget the grey-green eyes engraved in his memory. The new life he had constructed for himself was as intricate, elegant, and fascinating as any of his buildings. Paris, the Isle of Capri, San Francisco, Manhattan, Chicago, what did any of those moments with any of those women mean?

He had all the trappings of worldly success, but he wasn't happy. Numbly, he placed the ring in his inside pocket. His fingers encountered the third envelope — the Great Barrier Reef. A wry smile curled his lips and he ran his fingers through his thick, dark hair. What was he going to do now?

"Ashton, are you sure? Why don't you reconsider?"

"No. Thanks for the offer, Brent. It's terribly kind of you, considering everything I've just hit you with." He was sitting on the edge of the couch, dressed casually in faded jeans and a tweed sports jacket. An errant lock of golden hair fell across his forehead. He was trying so hard to be cheerful for her sake, but Ashton knew that their morning's conversation had been a terrible blow to him.

"Thanks for lunch. It was good to laugh a little."

"The pleasure was mine. Ashton, we'd have a wonderful time exploring some of Sydney together. Melbourne is only an hour away by plane; we could even go there if you like." He was so earnest, so eager to please.

"No. I think I just need to spend some time by myself. I need to find me again, discover who I am. You were right when you said I'd stopped living."

"I didn't mean to hurt you. I was angry. I'm sorry if I overstepped the mark."

"It's okay, Brent. Those things needed to be said. It takes courage to speak the truth. I actually don't know how you've managed to be silent all these years."

"I guess I just hoped that you would snap out of it. Hoped that if I loved you enough, you might realize one day. . . ."

"Well I realize now." Ashton spoke quietly, gently. "I'm sorry it's not quite the outcome that you had in mind."

Brent just smiled at her sadly as she continued, "When do you have to be back at work?"

"Not till next week."

"Are you going to stay here?"

"Not without you. I think I'd rather go home. What about you? What are your plans?"

"I made arrangements this morning to fly to the Great Barrier Reef."

"So, you'd made up your mind even before I got here?"

She nodded. "This is something I have to do. My plane leaves in three hours. I haven't even packed yet."

"I'll take that as a hint, shall I?" He stood, preparing to leave.

The kindness in her voice stopped him. "Brent, thank you for being here. I didn't want it to be this way, but I couldn't have known it would be like this. Am I making any sense?"

Swallowing the lump in his throat, he answered, "Yeah." He didn't want to torture either of them any further. "Do you need help with anything?"

Ashton looked around herself absently. "I don't think so. It won't take me long to get my things together:'

"Can I at least take you to the airport?"

Ashton shook her head.

"Not this time, Brent. Thanks."

"Will you at least call me if you need anything . . .anything at all?"

"Okay."

"Promise?"

"I promise."

He paused before the door. Turning to Ashton, he looked at her before embracing her tenderly. "Well, Sis, I'll see you when you get home."

Ashton felt her eyes welling with tears, as she looked into the face of this kind, generous man — her friend. She touched his face, feeling the hint of stubble beneath her fingers. "Brent, you'll find the right woman. I just know you will. You're too special."

He took her hand in his, holding it for a moment, before lowering it from his face.

"Not now, Ashton. Not now."

And with that he was gone, closing the door silently behind him.

"Don't you think you've had enough?" The bartender stood in his crisp white shirt, arms folded, waiting patiently for a response. There was almost a look of pity on his kind, creased face as he regarded the dejected man slumping over the bar. "Sir, you've been drinking for two hours solid How about taking a break?"

"I'm f-f-f-fine. Give me another of the same."

The bartender paused, pondering the wisdom of this latest request, before pouring another bourbon. He set the glass carefully on the counter, in front of the blonde haired man now supporting the weight of his head in his hands. He looked like he hadn't slept in three days.

"Your drink, Sir."

Brent looked up blearily. "Thanks. Just put it on my tab."

Nodding, the bartender added jovially, "You look like you've had a really tough day, but how about we make this the last one? You'll probably thank me for it tomorrow."

"I don't care about tomorrow."

"Cheer up, Mate. Life can't be that bad."

Brent thought for a moment, lost in a reverie, before asking, "Have you ever been in love?"

"Oh, I should have guessed. A woman, huh? They'll do it to you every time."

Brent's eyes were glazed as he leaned closer to confide in the bartender.

"This was no ordinary woman."

"No, they never are," came the dry response.

Brent swayed slightly. "Are you making f..fun of me?"

"Me? Wouldn't dream of it. I've just seen this too many times before."

"There will never be another woman for me . . . Haven't you ever been in love?"

"Sure."

"And . . .?"

"They were some of the best and the worst moments of my life."

"Well, what happened to her?"

"I married her!" The old man broke into uproarious laughter.

"Lucky you."

The bartender smiled and began polishing the glasses.

Brent continued, droning pitifully to nobody. "You know, I was so sure she would marry me. I've loved her all my life. I never thought she would say no, especially after he died." There was a tone of sarcasm in his voice now. "God, that was ten years ago."

The bartender cocked an eyebrow in interest. "And just what happened ten years ago?"

"This guy she was going out with — he was killed in a car accident. She never got over it, she's been pining for 'im all these years. And I've been waiting for her . . .like a damned fool."

The waiter let out a low whistle, "Boy, that's a tough break."

Chapter Twenty-One

Karl Van Ness walked into the bar of the Osprey Hotel. He didn't usually frequent bars, but he had spent an ineffectual morning surrounded by plans and sketches with little to show for it. All he could see was Ashton's face every time he tried to make a mark on the paper. This now seemed like a good place of refuge, as good as any.

He sauntered to the mahogany bar, moving with the grace of a wild animal. His steely blue gaze automatically noticed the two women sitting in a comer by the bay windows. They smiled, as he nodded his head in acknowledgment. He didn't feel like talking.

He waited, hands spread flat against the wood of the bar counter, as if drawing strength from it. The bartender was watching over a drunk fellow, draped across the counter a few chairs away. The barman looked at Karl, gestured at the drunk, and shrugged his shoulders. He nodded in understanding as Karl lifted his hand and signaled for a drink.

"Looks like you've got your hands full." Karl gestured towards the inebriated Brent as the bartender handed him his Dalwhinne on the rocks.

"Yeah, poor guy's having girl problems." Karl merely frowned.

"He's taking it really badly — she doesn't want to marry him. Still, guess that's life huh? Let me know if you need anything else, Sir."

Karl nodded, wondering what it was that made people spill their guts to complete strangers. He was staring into his drink, listening to the ice clink against the crystal, when Brent's voice intruded upon his thoughts.

"She doesn't want to marry me. She's not going to marry him, but she doesn't want to marry me. Try 'n explain that! She ss . . .says she loves me like a brother. She's been in love with him all this time. I never had a chance . . .she's been in love with a dead man all this time. How can anybody — I don't care how great they are — compete with a dead man? . . .Huh?"

Karl's heart skipped a beat. He turned his head slowly, fixing the stare of his eyes upon the rambling Brent, looking at him properly for the first time since he had entered the room.

His jaw twitched slightly as Brent continued, "That's the worst part. She's in love with a man who's been dead for over ten years . . . s-s-s-shc thinks he's alive. She thinks he didn't die. Isn't that ridiculous? She's crazy."

He paused, swaying slightly, as Karl and the bartender watched silently. He continued talking to his bourbon. "But I know he died. I know he died in that car crash. Her father told me. The hospital said it was all over. They said he was dead. How can he be alive now? She's so beautiful, but she's still crazy."

Karl leapt from his bar stool. In two strides he was beside Brent's sagging figure. "Who are you talking about?" It wasn't so much a question as a command.

Brent lurched around to find Karl's fiery eyes boring into him. He would have been startled, but the alcohol had made him oblivious to most of his surroundings. He slurred, "And w-w-who are you?"

"Never mind" Karl struggled to contain his impatience and the urge to shake this man by his shoulders. "Please tell me who you're talking about."

"My girl. Except she's not my girl — she never has been."

"What's her name?"

"Oh, it's a beautiful name . . . her name . . . say, do ya wanna have a drink?"

"What is her name?" Karl demanded again.

"Oh, her. Her name is . . . Ashhhton."

Karl stood dumbly looking at Brent in disbelief. He whispered hoarsely, "And the man she thought was dead?" He didn't need the answer, but he wanted to hear it said, wanted to hear the words come alive in the air.

"Do we have to talk about him?" reeled the drunk Brent.

Karl shook him fiercely, "Say it. What was his name?"

"Ryan. Ryan Brooks . . .ssss. Though he is not Ryan anymore. I don't know. He's somebody else, but it's still him. I don't know. I don't know anything anymore."

Karl let go of Brent's jacket. He didn't realize he'd grabbed it.

"Oh my God, what have I done? Ashton my darling, what have I done?"

Turning to the bartender he asked quickly, "Do you have any chilled Veuve Clicquot?"

"Yes, Sir."

"Give me a bottle right now."

Taking the bottle from the barman he turned to Brent and looked at him with compassion.

"Thanks."

As Karl strode from the bar, he could still hear Brent's voice rambling aimlessly.

Karl stopped outside the door to Ashton's suite in an attempt to steady his nerves. He glanced down at his grey knit shirt and black slacks, brushing them off nervously, though there was nothing to brush. The bottle of champagne rested in the curve of his arm like a sleeping baby. He raised a trembling fist to the door and knocked. He stood waiting, every second an eternity.

He was about to knock again, when the door opened hesitantly. Karl looked upon a face he did not recognize.

"I beg your pardon. I was looking for Ms. Ashton Cameron. This is her room, isn't it?"

The door swung back fully to reveal an aproned house maid. She stepped back as he walked slowly into the room. The scent of Ashton's perfume hung in the air.

"Oh, yes Sir, this was her room, but she checked out a few hours ago."

"I see." He spoke dully, as the color drained from his face. The room seemed lifeless to him now. Walking to the window, he gazed upon the sheet of glass that was the harbor, oblivious to the eyes of the maid fixed upon him. He stood silently for a few moments, unable to move. Finally, he held up the bottle of champagne and spoke to it. "I guess I'll have no use for you now."

"Are you all right?" The maid was frowning, slightly concerned.

"Here, why don't you have this." He turned suddenly and gave her the bottle. "You'll probably enjoy it more than I will right now."

"Why, thank you, Sir."

"Have a good day."

"You too," she said as he stalked silently from the room. "What a nice man."

Chapter Twenty-Two

Ashton was just crossing the foyer, the porter with her bags in tow, when she was greeted by the sight of Evelyn coming through the hotel's main entrance. It was impossible for the women to avoid each other.

"Good afternoon, Evelyn."

Evelyn's face revealed her genuine surprise. "Ashton, are you leaving us?"

"Yes, Evelyn. Congratulations, you finally get what you've been after all along!"

"What are you talking about?"

"You know very well what I'm talking about. He's all yours. I'm leaving." Ashton's eyes flashed with a quiet dignity, "You wouldn't understand."

Evelyn returned Ashton's gaze, not with anger, but with a warmth and gentleness that Ashton hadn't expected. She took Ashton gently by the arm. "No, my dear. I think it's you who do not understand. My driver will take you to the airport, and I shall explain a few things on the way."

"But . . ." Ashton began to protest, but the kindness in Evelyn's demeanor stopped her. It was so unexpected it took her by surprise. "Thank you."

Comfortably ensconced in the back of Evelyn's silver-gray Mercedes, Ashton felt numb. It was Evelyn who took charge and gave her chauffeur the directions. Voice as smooth as silk she purred, "John, Kingsford-Smith airport, Qantas please."

With a nod of his head, they were underway. Turning her attention to Ashton, Evelyn began, "Ashton honey, I think you have a mistaken idea of the relationship between Karl and me. It's true that I am very close to him. Perhaps as close as he has allowed any human being to be, since you, all those years ago. After the accident, he couldn't comprehend that you weren't there."

"But I didn't know." Ashton interjected.

"I suspected as much. Tell me, my dear, what happened?"

"I woke up after three days, and they were all standing around me. I remember the look on their faces. When I spoke they were all so amazed that I was okay. I ached everywhere, but apart from that I was fine. Then my Dad took my hand, and said,

"Princess, we're awfully happy to have you back." I searched all the faces but he wasn't there. My heart sank, Evelyn, their faces told me what I feared — he was dead. I tried to ask, but I couldn't stop crying. Brent was there holding my hand, and I begged him with my eyes to tell me the truth. I remember, he shook his head, "Yes honey, he's gone."

Evelyn's eyes were filled with tears as she sat silent, listening.

Ashton continued, "After I left the hospital, we never spoke about the accident again. My parents never mentioned if the police had given them my duffel bag, if they knew that I was eloping with Ryan that night. We never spoke about it."

Ashton looked out the window. "They'd been trying to send me to finishing school in Europe for a long time, thinking that time away from Ryan would change how I felt about him. I had been fighting them every step of the way. Suddenly, there was no more reason to fight. So, I went to Europe, and the rest, as they say, is history."

"Ashton, I'm so sorry. But you have to understand that nothing happens without a purpose, and although you have both been through an enormous amount of pain, the growth you have experienced because of it has made you the rather extraordinary human beings you are today."

She paused momentarily, reflecting on her own rite of passage. "Synchronicity is perhaps beyond our understanding, but it nevertheless exists. The Ryan you and I knew all those years ago was a kind, sensitive, talented, intelligent young man, with an enormous amount of potential. And that's the key word, potential.

He didn't have your social education, or background, or the drive that you've always had inside of you. He might have become an architectural firm's assistant, or a bohemian artist, living in Venice Beach in sunny California. Ashton, because of what happened, and only because of that, Karl Van Ness is the man he is today."

"Oh, but Evelyn, I loved Ryan so."

"I know you did, darling. And he loved you, too. But if you look deep in your heart, don't you know that the young man Ryan was could never have fulfilled all the woman that you are? He could have never held your interest year after year."

Ashton looked out of the window, unwilling for Evelyn to see the tears welling in her eyes. "You see . . ." she placed her hand on Ashton's shoulder, "And now I get to the part about our relationship, Karl's and mine. I recall the one thing that pulled me to him. What I mentioned to you before — his potential. That's always been one of my greatest faults," she smiled at herself, "And perhaps one of my greatest virtues. I've always loved taking care of people. When Branford, my husband, died, I was left with an enormous amount of money and an enormous amount of time, and nobody to take care of.

When I learned what had happened to Ryan, I remembered how much Branford talked of his skill with such great pride. Remembering that he had no family, I thought it was the perfect time to don my angel wings and fly to his side."

She laughed softly. "Ashton, it helped heal the ache, the emptiness inside of me, as I tried to help him come back to life. You see, Branford had been everything to me. There wasn't a moment we didn't spend together. And now here was someone who had no one, just like me. Do you understand now?"

Ashton nodded.

"I think I'm beginning to see."

"Ashton, it's been such a joy to see Ryan, or I should say Karl, grow into this splendid man, bursting with energy, filled with creativity, realizing his full potential.

But remember, Ashton dear, he has never loved anyone but you, and he still does."

"Well, he sure doesn't act like it."

"Ashton, don't you know how prideful he can be? Are you sure you want to get on this plane? We can turn the car around, you know?"

"Evelyn, I've tried every way I know how, to scale those magnificent walls he has constructed. There is simply no way around, over, or through them. He simply won't hear of it. He doesn't want to know. And I really don't know what is more painful. Being in love with a ghost, or loving a man who is dead to his true feelings. I can't live like this anymore. I have to get on with my life. I love him. I love him more than anything. But you know something, I love me too. I'm leaving for the health of my own heart."

"I respect your feelings, Ashton. It takes some people their entire lives and they never learn to love themselves. I respect you very much, and my best wishes go with you."

She reached into her black alligator clutch and drew from it a gold card case. Handing Ashton her card, she added warmly, "Anytime you need me, you know where to find me."

Chapter Twenty-Three

Brent woke up in a darkened room with no idea where he was. He staggered out of bed and into the shower and stood there letting the water run over his body. He made it colder and colder until he shivered, but gradually his head cleared.

He looked at his computer and realized he had lost an entire day. He thought wryly, "I don't think I've ever been that drunk in my life." All he remembered was leaving Ashton and going down to the bar where he started drinking bourbon nonstop.

He checked his phone and called downstairs for his messages. There were two texts from his folks and a fax from his father's office. He let them know he was okay.

He ordered breakfast and sat looking out at the harbor and wondered about his next move. He thought, I guess it's time to give up Ashton once and for all. Maybe it's time to accept her as part of my life only as a family friend. But something inside kept pressing him to do more.

Brent called downstairs again and asked if Ashton Cameron was registered. Reception told him Ashton checked out the day before and left no forwarding contact information.

Despite the elegance of the breakfast tray, he could only force down a few bites of fresh melon and half a croissant. The coffee was just what he needed. He sat with his head in his hands, and he turned to pick up the phone and change his reservations to return to the US.

He stopped dead. "I can't give up that easily. I know who knows where she is — Ashton's father. Ashton's parents are part of my family, too."

"It's Brent. Yes, I'm still in Sydney and I was getting ready to come home. Yes, Ashton said she was going to the Reef. I have something important to ask you. Joe, you know how much I love your daughter."

"And I know she loves you too, Brent."

"Yeah, but the problem is, she doesn't love me the way I love her. I'm her best friend or her brother. But I just can't give up and I also want to be sure she's OK before I make a reservation to come home. I need to ask you — well, I know Ashton always lets you know where she is. I gotta give it one more try. Could you tell me where she is?"

"Well, son, if it were anybody else, I wouldn't do this. You know that Ashton's mom and I think of you as part of our family. We've been worried about Ashton. Frankly, nothing of what she's told us about this Karl person makes sense. I've got people on it who will find out more. Brent, we both wish you all the luck in the world. You know how much we love Ashton and both of us think you're the man who's a perfect match for our daughter."

He continued, "I'll text you the details. She's gone to a resort on the Great Barrier Reef. She told us she needed quiet and TLC and that she was fine. I was worried by the sound of her voice. It makes me happy that you're going to see her. Please, when you find out how she is . . .

please, please call, any time."

Brent felt a wave of relief course through his body. He packed quickly. He made new reservations and arranged for transport to the beachfront resort.

Suddenly, he was starving. He devoured the rest of his breakfast, called for a cab and was on the way to Cairns airport. A little later he was in Port Douglas. He checked in for a week, not knowing how long he and Ashton needed to talk, to listen, and to honor the friendship they had for most of their lives.

He was going to call Ashton's room, but decided instead he would write a note and leave it, so she had a little time to absorb the fact that he was there. He began to write, but after every few lines, he crumpled the paper and threw it out. Finally, he found the words.

Ashton came back to her room glowing from the sun and the ocean, but her heart was heavy. She stopped in front of the door when she saw an envelope peeking out. Her heart leapt in spite of herself, and she sighed when she recognized Brent's handwriting.

My dearest Ashton, forgive me, but I've loved you for too long to give up so easily. I called your dad, and he gave me the name of the resort where you were staying. He only did that because I'm part of your family. And as part of your family, I'm here if you need me at any hour. And I'm here, most of all, for us to talk about all we have meant to each other over the years. No matter what you decide, if it's only we're the best of friends, I'll respect your decision. You know how much I love you. Please, let's talk — heart-to-heart. How about dinner tonight? Let me know. Always, Brent.

Ashton's feelings were a jumble, and she didn't know how to respond. She just wanted to be left alone. But in the shower, holiday memories and family picnics, and times spent on the shore with her family and Brent flooded into her mind. They had known each other all their lives. Tears mingled with the water of the shower and soon she decided to see Brent. She felt the preciousness of the comfort and friendship he had always offered her.

She called the desk and left a message for Brent to call her. In a flash, the phone rang, and she heard the familiar warmth of his voice.

"Hey, sweet girl. Will you have dinner with me tonight?"

"Brent, I was mad . . . Well, I should be mad at you for showing up. I think I'm madder at my father for telling you where I was. She sighed. Yes, I'll have dinner with you."

"Oh Ashton, what ti . . . ?"

"Let me finish, Brent. But my request is, please, let's not talk about love or anything serious tonight. Let's just be. Can you do that? We'll talk about easy stuff — no drama. I'm too tired."

"Yes Ashton, I promise. How about 7 PM? In the dining room downstairs or out by the pool?"

"Yes, seven by the pool, that's great."

Ashton took a long shower, wrapped herself in a thick towel and lay down to relax a little. She hadn't been sleeping well at all.

She drifted off, and she kept seeing Karl's face, then Ryan's face. They blended into one, and still, those intense sapphire eyes stared at her, and those strong arms cradled her. The image seemed to move away, and she called his name and woke up with a start. Wow, she had been asleep for two hours, it was already 6 PM.

Ashton slipped into a cream and teal silk caftan and decided she didn't have the energy for makeup. A little light face oil, the Jurlique blend that had a heavenly fragrance, and some lip gloss. She combed her hair back into a ponytail, slipped some gold hoops in her ears and she was ready for dinner.

She caught sight of herself in the mirror, and she almost didn't recognize herself. There was a new look in her eyes. There was a new maturity and a deeper calm than she had ever seen.

She still had a few minutes, and she grabbed her journal and wrote.

Oh, I wish I knew what was going to happen with my life. I know I have a choice, but please help me to make the right choice. I am so grateful to be loved. I am grateful for my wonderful family. I'm grateful for this loving man downstairs waiting for me. I just feel grateful. Well, for a writer, that's pretty inarticulate, but it'll have to do for now. That's how I feel.

Chapter Twenty-Four

She walked slowly down the stairs in her jeweled sandals, the ones she bought in Sydney just before going on the boat with Karl. She didn't even know what she felt anymore. It certainly couldn't be love; she hurt too much. And anyway, if it was love, she didn't want any part of it.

She stopped and scanned the few people near the pool. At the tables set up for dinner closer to the ocean, she spotted Brent, sandy blonde hair falling over his forehead. He radiated health and vibrancy.

"What a beautiful man," Ashton thought. "What's the matter with me? Why am I stuck in a dream that turned into a nightmare? Angels, please give me wisdom."

Brent turned; his heart leapt when he saw her.

"Ashton, darlin', you look beautiful."

Her reply made him laugh.

"So, sadness becomes me? Just like the song, moonlight becomes me?"

"Ashton, if you were in a potato sack, you'd be gorgeous. Period. You know that."

"Brent," she put her hand over his and said very gently, "I didn't expect to feel this way. But the fact that you're here beside me, as my friend and with no expectations, but here, means more to me than I can say. Thank you, Brent."

"Ashton, that's one thing I can promise you, no matter what happens with us going forward, I am always here for you in any way that I can be. You're part of my

155

life and you're part of my heart. That won't change no matter what."

The server interrupted them and rattled off the specials.

Ashton said, "I'll have the fresh salad with prawns and Chevre and sparkling water with lime." Brent ordered the broiled snapper and veggies.

Asked if they would like a bottle of wine, Brent shook his head saying, "Right now, I can't even smell alcohol, or I'll be sick." He looked toward Ashton and her answer was no as well.

Before long, they were both talking easily about anything and everything. They relaxed into comfort. The sky was ablaze with the sunset, and the gorgeous colors were reflected in the surf.

"Ashton, do you remember when we all went down the shore to Long Beach Island? Those fabulous crabs we had at Joe's?"

"Yes, I remember."

"Remember the white house your folks rented, right on the ocean?"

"I remember when I won the ping-pong tournament!"

"Excuse me, young lady, excuse me — you didn't win the tournament, I did!"

Ashton laughed, and said, "I thought I could trick you into remembering it my way."

"Oh, Ashton, are you really glad I'm here? You looked so sad the last time I saw you."

"Brent, yes, I feel like part of my family is here now."

Seeing the sadness in her eyes, Brent's voice was warm and kind. "Ashton, I am part of your family, I'm part of your team. That's not going to change, it's here to stay. You can take that to the bank."

They became comfortably silent and listened to the murmur of the waves lapping on the shore. Ashton ordered fresh berries for dessert.

"I didn't realize I was hungry. That was so good."

"Want to go for a walk?" Brent pulled back her chair and they easily moved into sync as they walked down to the shore. Ashton removed her teal blue Amalfi sandals. The delicate Italian leather wasn't meant for sand or water.

"Brent, do you remember when Pogo discovered the ocean?" They both laughed.

The memory was a precious one. Ashton's birthday gift from Brent was an adorable white ball of fluff that she immediately named Pogo because he jumped instead of walking. The Shi-Tzu was a baby, fascinated by everything he discovered. He would let out an excited yelp and run back to Ashton to share his find. When Pogo saw the ocean for the first time, he rushed to the shore and stopped dead just before he touched the water. He ran back to Ashton yipping excitedly. She followed him down to the shoreline, where he played tag with the waves.

"Life was a lot simpler then, wasn't it, Ashton?'

"That's for sure, you had two more years at Princeton. And I was finishing up Journalism at Bryn Mawr. Do you remember, Brent, when we gave your mother that beautiful garden fairy for Christmas and we decorated her with tiny lights? There was snow everywhere. You told her Santa had left something in her garden."

"Yup, it was the first time in a couple of years the color returned to her cheeks. It made her so happy. The chemo was so intense, and she was gone by spring. Mom loved seeing that sprite in her precious garden. It's still there."

Ashton reached out and put her hand on Brent's shoulder. "Your mom was some special lady, Brent."

"Yeah, I still miss her. She sure knew how to let somebody know she loved them."

They walked quite a way up the beach, stopping and talking, simply two friends from childhood. Ashton began yawning and Brent asked, "Am I boring you?"

"No," Ashton laughed, "but all of a sudden, I'm so tired."

"Okay, sweet one, let's get ourselves back to the hotel." They walked in silence, broken only by the soft lapping of the waves against the shore.

"I'll walk you to your room." He kissed Ashton on her forehead and said, "Remember I'm a phone call away. I'm here for you at any hour."

"Thanks, Brent. I know you are."

Chapter Twenty-Five

When Ashton opened her computer, she was startled to find it was already 9:30 PM, but it was 11 AM in Connecticut. She dashed off an email to her Dad and let him know that she was doing so much better. She thanked him for letting Brent know where she was.

"You know, it's the strangest thing, but I feel as though part of my family is here. You're a wise man, Dad, and I love you. Give Mom a hug for me and save one for yourself.

P.S. I will finish the interview with Karl Van Ness. I haven't completed editing yet, but I'll have it to you by the end of the week as agreed."

She stepped out of the silky caftan and slipped into the pearl gray bias La Perla nightgown she loved so much. She rinsed her face and brushed her teeth. She smoothed on some Aveda body oil that made her skin feel heavenly. She slid into the luxurious sheets and before she knew it, she was fast asleep.

Ashton was walking on a path lined with trees. The full moon bathed everything in a magical light. Coming toward her was a handsome young man, tall and slender, with a backpack and an art storage tube. This felt like so many years ago. As he came closer, they locked eyes, and Ashton felt her stomach flutter with nervousness. He had the bluest eyes she'd ever seen. She asked in a timid voice, "Who are you?" But he just kept walking and didn't hear her. She turned to follow him, but he had disappeared into the trees. She started running and calling out, "Who are you? Who are you? I need to know."

Ashton woke up with a start. Her heart was beating so fast she could barely breathe. The person in her dream looked like the Ryan Brooks that she'd met years ago.

"Wow, 4:45 AM, well, I guess I'm getting up."

She drank some cool water and went to sit on her balcony. Her heart settled down, and the stars were so close, she could almost touch them. Her mind drifted back to the first time she met Ryan.

Ashton remembered loving the smell of the books in the Bryn Mawr library. Ashton was looking for *Cyrano de Bergerac* in French for her Literature class. In a hurry, she ran right into a young man with an arm full of books. He dropped the books. She muttered, "Excuse me," picked up her book, and ran back to the table. She looked down at the book only to find it was the wrong book. Ashton went back to the aisles and found the young man stacking books into a library cart.

"Excuse me — I am so sorry again. I didn't mean to run into you."

"Yeah? I didn't know there was a fire somewhere."

"Well, I'm sure there is a fire, somewhere. I picked up one of your books instead. Could you give me mine?"

She looked up into his eyes and felt this strange sensation. They were the bluest eyes she'd ever seen. But a deep blue, almost like sapphires. She felt herself blush and she was instantly annoyed with herself.

"Oh, this is a good one," he said handing her the book. "You can run into me anytime, especially in the pursuit of a good book."

"Thanks, but I don't think I'll take you up on that." Ashton laughed and tried to cover her discomfort.

"Too bad, I would enjoy it."

"Yeah, I bet you would."

"Hey, let's stop the sparring, and call a truce. I'm Ryan Brooks, who are you?"

"I'm Ashton. Ashton Cameron."

"Well, Ashton Cameron, it's a real pleasure to meet you – now maybe – maybe, I ought to get back to work."

Ryan watched her walk away, "There's something special about that girl. She's a lot more than pretty."

Ashton drifted out of her memories. She could see the dawn beginning to color the sky. Delicate fingers of violet gave way to lavender. Pink and orange colored the clouds. What a gorgeous time of the morning. She loved the dawn.

As Ashton did a couple of yoga stretches, a beautiful idea floated into her head. She called the concierge and booked a massage, a seaweed wrap, a facial and a mani-pedi at the Sunset Spa. Time for a little first-class self-care.

She left a message for Brent, he was probably still asleep. "I've gone for a swim and then a couple of treatments at the Spa. I need to take this day for myself,

Brent. I've been through a lot and it's time for a little nurturing."

The ocean was heavenly and refreshing. Ashton swam a few laps and then floated, watching the sun wake up the world around her. By the time she got back to the room and showered, there was a message from Brent, "Nurturing? I'm darned good at nurturing. Why don't we have a fun day, just relaxing?"

She rang his room, and he answered with a bright, "'Nurturing R Us,' what can we do for you, ma'am?"

"Oh Brent, you're a wonderfully silly man. Nope, today is all mine. I've booked yummy spa treatments. I'm going to be a new woman tomorrow."

"A new woman? But I like the old one. Okay, okay, I surrender, have a beautiful day. And hey, Ashton, I'll say it again, you know I'm here if you need me."

Ashton finished her green tea, along with pawpaw with a squeeze of lime, and a simple two-egg omelet. She wrote a couple of lines in her journal.

I am proud of myself of myself for paying attention to my heart and body, my needs and wants. Today isn't about anybody but me and I intend to enjoy every minute!

She closed her journal with a snap. She was ready for pampering. Ashton slipped into soft yoga pants, a halter top and a cuddly pink jacket that felt like a hug.

Chapter Twenty-Six

When Ashton stepped into the Sunset Spa, it felt like some sort of dream world. The lighting was soft with salt lamps and plants everywhere, and a beautiful, diffused scent was grounding and intoxicating all at the same time.

"Hi Ms. Cameron, I'm Ingrid, your guide for an afternoon of supreme relaxation. I promise you that when you walk out of here, you'll be a whole new woman. Follow me and I'll give you a little tour."

The layout of the spa was a tropical oasis. Everything in it, the colors, the textures were designed for relaxation and nurturing. Ashton smiled to herself, "This was a smart choice, girlfriend."

"This is our cold plunge pool."

"Oooo not for me, I like warm!"

"Then, I've got it — our saltwater float. Heavenly!"

"Yes, that's more like it."

"This is your locker. Wrap your hair up and slip into this robe and I'll bring you to Alla for your massage prep. Hop into the steam shower for about 10 to 15 minutes, a quick rinse, and that will prepare you for your exfoliation. I'll come get you."

And true to her word, Ingrid showed up bringing cool lemon water.

"Oh Ingrid, that is so refreshing and the lemon rind curls are lovely."

"Beauty refreshes the eyes, the mind and the spirit."

They walked through long hallways lined with beautiful art on the walls. "Ms. Cameron, this is Alla."

"Well, hello there sweetie, aren't you a pretty thing? I'll just step out. Slip off your robe, and lie face down." Alla was a short, slender woman probably in her 60s, with the gentlest voice.

Ashton removed the cuddly robe and climbed onto the table. Alla knocked softly and said, "Ms. Cameron, I use fine salt for exfoliation, but I think in your case it looks like you have sensitive skin, so if its ok with you, I'm going to change that to a more gentle sugar. Please guide me as to pressure and comfort."

"Oh Alla, yes, I do have sensitive skin. And it's a little on the dry side."

"Okay, I will use the sugar with the sweet almond oil." Alla began stroking Ashton's back and shoulders with the sugar and almond oil. "May I add a couple of drops of lavender for relaxation?"

"Oh yes," Ashton murmured. "That would be heavenly."

Alla stroked one side of Ashton's torso and rinsed her off with warm water and then placed a towel on that side. Ashton was smoothed with the sugar, rinsed lovingly and covered with a warm towel.

"Now lovely, turn over and I'll do the rest."

Ashton drifted in and out of a dreamlike state. She felt as though all her old self was being gently washed away. All the cares and sadness were finding their way down the drain.

While Alla was finishing her feet, she said, "Ms. Cameron I know you booked a seaweed wrap next, but might I suggest going right to your aromatherapy massage after your rain shower?"

"I felt a couple of tight spots in your shoulder blades, your neck, and in the small of your back, I suggest we do some deep massage along with soothing Swedish at the end. And I think 90 minutes, not 60. I feel that you've been through a lot, young lady, and I have the magic to make you feel better."

Ashton gratefully shook her head and padded into the rain shower. She washed away the last traces of sugar and the almond oil and her skin felt like warm silk. She felt all new.

Ingrid led her into another beautifully lit room filled with healing plants. Alla appeared with a rain stick; the soothing sounds made Ashton drift away.

Alla added two drops of lavender essential oil, a drop of geranium and sandalwood for grounding to the massage cream. As Allah's strong hands worked on the back of her neck and her shoulders, Ashton felt hot tears rise and she began to cry. She apologized and Alla said, "Darling, it's okay I had a feeling you needed this. It's OK, cry. It's okay, you are safe."

Ashton couldn't stop crying and she felt like a small child. Gradually, she allowed in the comfort and safety, and soon she breathed softly in that netherworld between wakefulness and sleep.

She awoke to Alla saying gently, "Turn over, my dear."

Ashton felt like she couldn't move, her body was so heavy and relaxed.

Alla continued the incredible massage, ending with the effleurage of gentle strokes. Ashton was transported to a place of such relaxation and peace. "I don't think I felt this deeply relaxed in years, Alla."

"I'm so happy to be of service." Alla replied, "Slip into this caftan and Ingrid will come and get you for a very light lunch, after you rest for about 30 minutes."

Ashton was shown to the atrium where a small fountain was murmuring and was cuddled into a swing lined with soft cushions. She drifted into deep relaxation, and then suddenly, in the mist of the fountain, she saw Karl's face. He was so close and yet so distant. She felt such pain in her heart, such longing and great sadness.

A woman she hadn't seen before brought a little tray of beautiful fruit, macadamia nuts and a fragrant chai tea.

Her soft voice inquired, "Would you like anything more before I bring you to the facial room?"

"No thank you. I'm ready."

Ashton was amazed as she followed her guide, who seemed to move on little cat feet. She took in and embraced the silence of the place broken only by occasional chimes, the fragrance of the most delicate incense, and the movement of gentle waters. What a soul-healing place.

Ashton was escorted to a chair that felt like she was lying on clouds. The woman who worked on her face,

Annie, had small hands that massaged and kneaded her jaw, the area around her eyes, and her neck. The potions she used were gentle and infused moisture into every pore.

Another girl polished and filed the tips of her nails perfectly, echoing the shape of her cuticles. No pointed or square-shaped nails for her. Ashton was an expert in harmonizing with her own beauty. Another woman worked on her pedicure. Ashton chose a soft translucent shell pink for fingertips and toes. Both women were delighted with the choice of color.

When she finished the facial, Annie misted her face with a natural spray scented with rose attar. Ashton was handed a mirror, and the face that looked back at her, this relaxed young woman, felt almost like a stranger. She thanked everyone and slipped back into her yoga pants, halter top, and cuddly pink jacket.

Ashton couldn't believe it was almost sunset, time to have a light dinner sent up to her room and to mull over the tumble of thoughts that had flown into her heart and mind on this delicious day.

When she got to her room, there was the most perfect small jasmine bouquet from Brent. The simple note read: *A perfect ending to a perfect day. May you have the sweetest dreams tonight, Ashton.*

Ashton left a message for Brent with reception: *Thanks, dear Brent, the flowers are lovely, and yes, I had the most wonderful day. See you tomorrow for breakfast.*

Ashton sat on the balcony and watched the moonrise. It was only 8 PM, but she knew she was going to sleep.

Chapter Twenty-Seven

Ashton woke up to the colors of the sunrise lighting the morning sky. She stretched and had a smile on her face just like that scene in *Gone with the Wind*, when Scarlett O'Hara awakened in bed feeling loved. It made Ashton laugh out loud — well, this time there was no Rhett Butler who ravished me. This time the lover was me for me! I truly took care of myself yesterday. An entire day all about me. Oh, I feel wonderful.

Her skin was silken, and her energy was off the charts. She put on her beige yoga pants with an eyelet swing jacket over a bright pink and gold bathing suit. She popped her hair into a shining ponytail. She put on sunblock, her facial oil, some lip gloss, and she was ready for breakfast — she was starving.

She rang Brent's room and realized it was only 7 AM. A sleepy voice answered the phone. "Hey Brent, wake up, the sun is shining!"

"Yeah, but I was sleeping."

"Come on sleepyhead, it's time for breakfast. I'm going downstairs. I'm starving so I'm going to order, do you want croissants?"

"Yes, OK, see you in a bit."

She flew down the stairs in golden sandals and picked a table closest to the shore.

"Good morning Mark, my friend is joining me shortly. I'd love a cappuccino with an espresso shot and some croissants to start."

Ashton watched the gentle waves rolling in, the sunlight sparkling on the water and thought, no matter what I've gone through, I'm fine. I love my life and I am so filled with gratitude. All is well. I'm going to be fine. And then out loud she said quietly, "Angels, thank you for this beautiful day."

"Well, is there anything I can do to make this day even more beautiful for you, Ms. Cameron?" She looked into Brent's laughing face. His blonde hair was tousled, his eyes were still sleepy, and his voice so warm and kind.

"How about these gorgeous croissants? Do you want coffee or cappuccino or a cappuccino with a shot?"

"Sounds good. Well, look at you. What did you do to yourself? Missy, you look like a shining little kid. You're glowing — wow! Is that what a spa day does for you? And I bet I have something that's going to make you glow, too. He reached into the pocket of his linen jacket and took out a brochure. I was going to book this, but I wanted to make sure you liked the idea."

"How about a full day tomorrow on a glass-bottom catamaran that goes around the Great Barrier Reef? A chef makes a great lunch, there's snorkeling, and swimming. Or we can just relax on board. You can watch turtles, fish, and coral. . . . What do you think? Does that sound good to you?"

"That sounds great, Brent. Yes, make reservations. It sounds like a perfectly wonderful day."

"Okay done. I must have caught it from you, I'm hungry, too. How about an omelet? Sound good? Mark, a couple of omelets and papaya with lime — oops, I mean pawpaw. I'll be right back. I'll make the reservations, and how about two lounges under big umbrellas for the day? What do you say?"

"Yes, Brent but you better hurry up 'cause I'm hungry enough to eat both omelets!"

Ashton buttered her second croissant as Mark brought the omelets and Brent arrived smiling from ear to ear. "Thank goodness I arrived in time, or the glowing sea monster would've devoured my omelet."

They finished with the glorious papaya. Easy and comfortable, they talked about home, and Ashton mentioned she needed to finish editing the interview with Karl Van Ness.

Brent's blue eyes got cloudy, and he frowned, "Ashton, isn't that going to be awfully hard on you?"

"Yes, it won't be easy, but I promised my dad and after all, I'm a pro. When you say you're going to do a job, you complete it."

"Ashton, I love that about you. I love that you're passionate about your work. We're awfully lucky, you know. We both have work that we love. That makes for an easy relationship.

Ashton raised her eyebrows.

"Don't raise your eyebrows at me, it's the truth, and you know it. Well, that was delicious. How about heading over to our umbrellas?"

"Yes, sounds perfect, all I need to do is take off my jacket and put on sunscreen."

They strolled together laughing, comfortable, two people who really know each other. There were two chaise lounges with a protective sun umbrella that looked like half of a nautilus shell. They had their own little cave complete with plush towels and bottles of water and juice in an ice bucket.

Ashton stood up to go into the water, her hot pink print with gold one-piece suit with high cut legs and a deep V-neck made heads swivel!

Brent uttered a low whistle," Wow, that bathing suit is hot stuff – no, correction – you're hot stuff, Ashton!"

"Come on, lazybones, I'll beat you to the water." As they both ran laughing into the ocean, Ashton realized there was still a lot of little kid in both of them when they were around each other. They were the same age, with such a similar background.

Karl, on the other hand. Why did she have to think about that now? Karl, on the other hand, didn't have to say a word. When he looked at her, there was no 'wow' in words, there was a burning sensuality that enveloped them. No, I'm not going to think about it now. She splashed Brent and he splashed her right back.

The water was translucent and she floated effortlessly.

"Stop thinking about Karl. Stay present, Ashton. Be smart Ashton. This man loves you. You know him. He knows you — it's easy, isn't it? There are no lies, no hiding. Ashton, wise up girl."

Brent swam up behind her and put his hand under the back of her head pulling her in a wide circle, "Doesn't that feel great, honey?"

Ashton relaxed. The sun was ablaze, and both retreated to the shade of their beach oasis. Ashton had some water. Brent did too.

"Ashton, I gotta ask you. What happened? Have you really left this Karl guy? Is he really Ryan?" Brent spoke very gently. "Honey, I don't want to upset you, but I also want to understand what happened. I want to be there for you. Can we talk a little bit about it?"

"Brent, thank you for being so gentle. Yes, and you're right, no matter what happens between us, we are best friends, and I know we will always be. Yes, in many ways Karl Van Ness bears no resemblance to Ryan. He is shorter, he's hardened not just his body, but his heart. He is convinced that I left him, that I just went on with my life after the accident."

"Brent, we were eloping that night. We were going to be married the night of the accident. Do you realize that Brent, we were going to be married?"

"No, honey, I didn't know. I was never really sure about any of it. I knew you loved him. Your parents didn't say anything to me, only that he died in the accident. Well, not even that, they just said, 'He didn't make it.' They said the same thing to you, right? All of us assumed he died."

"He did almost die Brent, and if it wasn't for Evelyn by his side, who had the resources to get the best in the medical field to put him back together again, he never would've survived. Who knows how many operations he's gone through? He only has traces of scars. Who knows the pain he suffered, the amount of plastic surgery, not just the reconstruction? More than the physical pain, he suffered the pain of thinking that the woman he loved, didn't love him. And he decided that when he saw me, he was going to get even."

"Yeah, but you didn't recognize him immediately?"

"No Brent. He's shorter than Ryan, he's muscular. His eyes are the same color, but certainly not the look in his eyes. Ryan was so — so – so sweet. This man is not sweet by a long shot. This is a man of the world – confident and sure of himself. This is no young student of architecture. His voice is different. It's husky. His face is completely different."

"Brent, I fell in love with a man that my soul knew, but in every other way, he was a stranger."

Tears scalded her cheeks. "I'm sorry Brent, I know this is hard to hear. But you're part of my family, and I really want you to know what happened. When I discovered he knew who I was and that this was an elaborate plan to get revenge, I hated him. But you know, hate isn't that far from love. I know that sounds crazy, but the opposite of love is indifference, not hate. I don't want to think of him, yet I. . . ." Her voice trailed off.

"Oh, honey, I feel how much you are hurting. I wish I could make it all go away but I know I can't. Only time will heal this, Ashton. I just want you to know I'm here for you no matter what."

"I know you are, Brent, and that means the world to

me." Suddenly, Ashton was exhausted, "I think I'll go up and take a nap."

"That sounds like a plan. Let's meet for dinner. How about six?"

"OK. Hey, Brent," Ashton put her hand on his arm, "Thank you for listening and for being such a wonderful friend."

Ashton went up to her room and took a long shower, mingling her tears with the water. Finally, she felt peaceful, slipped into the beautiful bed, and drifted into a light sleep.

There was a knock at the door, and Ashton opened it to find a beautiful little box with a note on top saying, "Some flowers for your hair." Tiny orchids. Ashton put them along the line of her French twist. She pulled out her bias green silk dress, slipped on her gold sandals and went down to meet Brent, ready for food, music, and some good company.

Chapter Twenty-Eight

Ashton's phone rang and her heart skipped a beat when she saw Evelyn's name, "Dear girl," murmured the soft voice, "I was wondering how you are. Talk to me."

"Oh Evelyn, I'm trying to sort through a million conflicting feelings. I don't even know what I feel anymore. Brent, my friend, really loves me — he really does — he's here with me and I'm realizing how much I love him."

"Love him?"

"Yes, Evelyn, well . . . yes, I love him. I've known him all my life. Our families are as close as blood relatives. I've known him since I was a little girl. He is so kind and so sweet, and he respects me and . . . and . . ."

"And. . . . He isn't Karl, is he?"

"Oh Evelyn, nobody is Karl, except Karl."

"I know, darling, I know. When Karl laid in that hospital bed, broken into what seemed a thousand pieces, you need to know that he kept asking for you."

Ashton felt the hot tears rise, "Evelyn, I didn't know. Believe me. I didn't know he was alive. I . . . I felt dead inside. My parents made all the arrangements and within a week after I got out of the hospital, I was at school in Switzerland and everything was strange and new and I felt totally alone. Oh Evelyn, how could my parents do this?"

"Darling Ashton, that's something I'm afraid we can't answer. They must've had profoundly serious reasons. He was Ryan, yes? Ryan Brooks. He is most definitely not the same man today. The first couple of weeks I didn't think he would make it. His doctors said it was touch and go."

"Evelyn, do you mind telling me what Ryan's, I mean Karl's, recovery was like?"

"He was still Ryan Brooks then. My husband had taken him under his wing and was so proud of his talent and design ideas. When Branford died, taking care of Ryan seemed to bring him back to me for a little while. I found the most incredible specialists, and they pieced Ryan back together bit by bit. The doctors weren't sure he'd be able to walk again, but I have never seen anyone so determined to come back, almost from the dead. He sweated and cried and dragged himself between those bars. He developed physical strength and had a will that I've never seen in anyone."

"You said he asked about me . . . talked about me."

"Finally, after many weeks, he asked again, "Have you heard from Ashton?" I choked up. I couldn't answer. He saw the tears in my eyes and that was the last time he asked about you. Many months into his healing he told me the story of how you met and that you were running away to be married."

Ashton sobbed quietly, unable to say a word.

"Ashton, my sweet, I hear you. This is truly a tragedy, what happened to the two of you. I think you were made for each other. But then consider this, my dear. Ryan Brooks was not raised like you, he didn't have the advantages you did. He was truly not part of your privileged world. Neither of us can say how your relationship would have evolved over the years. Karl Van Ness is far more of a match for the woman you are, Ashton. Do you know that in your heart?"

"Evelyn, I do . . . yes, part of me really understands that, but what seems impossible is how could he believe that I would've deserted him?"

"Sweetheart, you weren't there. You were not there during the most challenging journey of his life. You two were about to be married and suddenly you were simply gone. Understand how that must've felt to him."

Ashton couldn't speak, "Oh, Evelyn, I don't know what to do."

"Promise me only one thing, Ashton. Before you make any life-changing decisions, meet with Karl one more time."

Ashton was silent until at last, through her shuddering breath she said, "Yes, Evelyn, I do promise you that. No, I promise myself that. I was so angry and hurt when I left and felt that 'never' would be too soon to see him ever again. But, yes, I promise."

"Darling, take the time you need, and keep returning to the only thing that matters in this life – love. In the end, it is the only thing that matters. I know what I'm talking about. I was a successful woman and happy with my life.

When I met Branford, I discovered a new world that I didn't even know was possible and I treasured every moment we shared. Again, take all the time you need.

Call me anytime. I'm happy to know you better, Ashton. I can see why Karl loves you so much. Good night. We'll talk soon, yes?

"Thank you, Evelyn, really. Thank you, I never expected your kindness."

Ashton hung up and threw herself on the pillows and sobbed until it felt like she had no more tears left. She left a message for Brent that she had a bit of a headache and would have dinner in her room.

Ashton drew a warm bath and added four drops of lavender, three of sandalwood, two drops of geranium and a tablespoon of sweet almond oil. She stopped crying, and the warm water was such a comfort. The soothing scent made all her muscles feel loose.

She ate half her green salad and thought, "I think I need to sleep. Tomorrow will be much clearer." And just before she fell asleep, she felt as though those sapphire eyes were gazing down at her. "Good night, good night my darling Karl."

Chapter Twenty-Nine

When Ashton woke up, it seemed like something had changed. She wasn't sure what, but it seemed the sun was calling her out to play. She looked at the clock and was stunned to find it was already after 7:00 AM, super late for her. She rang Brent's room, but he wasn't there.

She put on her bathing suit and the lovely coral and white marbled silk caftan over it. She flew down the stairs and immediately saw Brent sitting at the table they had shared the other morning.

"Good morning, Sunshine, how did you sleep?'

"Do you know that I slept for 10 hours, Brent, that's unheard of for me."

"Well, with all the heavy thoughts in that beautiful head, it's no wonder you were tired. Your headache is gone, yes?"

"Yes, I feel lighter somehow, some clarity breaking through."

"Clarity about us?"

"Oh, that's a little heavy for breakfast conversation don't you think, Brent? "

"No, I think it's time we talked," he said gently. "Ashton, listen to me. I've known you forever and it seems like I've loved you forever — no matter how corny that sounds — so don't wrinkle your nose at me. I promised you I wouldn't hound you and I haven't. As it turns out, I've got to get back to the States, and I want once and for all, to tell you what's in my heart and let's see where this goes. Are you game?"

"You're right, Brent. You have been an absolute angel and a support. And I know you need to talk to me."

"Ashton, think of how easily our lives will mesh with each other? We don't have to make huge adjustments. I already know who you are and how you think, and you know the same about me. Most people who put their lives together don't know nearly what we know about each other."

"That's true." Ashton murmured and asked the waiter. "May I have a refill on the cappuccino and shot."

"You're right. We've said this before. Even when I walk with you, it's comfortable. It's natural, it's easy. But Brent, although I love you, I love you like family. You're part of my life, but I know that there's a different kind of love, because I've felt it."

"Is it possible, Ashton, that what you're feeling belongs to another time when you were much younger when you were enchanted with Ryan."

"Brent, it wasn't enchantment. We were going to be married, against everybody's wishes. Do you realize that? It was a big deal to know that I was going against what my parents wanted for me. We'd always been so close and all of a sudden, everything was different. Ryan was a gentle soul and we were so different but there was something that I admit I'd never felt before."

"Ashton. . . ."

Ashton put her hand gently on his arm, "Wait, let me finish. And then when I met Karl, his and my connection was deeper than anything I had ever experienced.

Maybe my heart understood what my brain couldn't comprehend, but all I know is that Karl is a strong man with incredible depth that Ryan never had."

"Yeah? Do you realize you're talking about the same man?"

"Am I really talking about the same man? Everything Evelyn told me is that the Ryan I knew is nowhere to be found in this man called Karl Van Ness. Brent, you have to believe me, this man was at death's door. The doctors had no hope. He was healed by a woman who believed in him, hired the best medical experts, and did everything in her power to help him survive."

"Yeah, and. . . ."

"Bitterness hardened his heart. He thought that the woman who was going to marry him didn't care enough to be by the side."

"Ashton, that's ridiculous. You know you would've been by his side. Whether we like it or not, and you know I love them, but your parents lied to you. I don't know how much they knew or when. I do know when they found out you were going to survive, that your injuries were minor, they immediately began a campaign to get you out of town. You know they did it with love."

"Was it really love Brent? Or was it 'we want you to do things our way and then we'll love you'?"

"You know your parents wanted more for you, Ashton. Ryan had nothing in this world, and they probably thought he was looking for financial comfort."

"You know it was the last thing on his mind."

"No, Ashton, I don't know anything of the sort. I didn't know the guy. But if you tell me that, I believe you. But put yourself in their shoes for a minute. This was a young man with no background, with no family who yes, had talent, but didn't seem very ambitious and certainly had none of the social graces that would've allowed him to integrate into your world easily."

"They lied to me Brent. I understand they had fears, but I wanted their support, not their lies. My entire world shifted when I realized what they did. Yes, it's true, I didn't investigate, but I was in no condition emotionally to investigate anything. In a way, I was grateful to go to another country with new surroundings and try to begin my world, my life, over again without Ryan. I felt like a grieving widow. "

Ashton's eyes were bright with tears and the look in Brent's eyes was compassionate. "Okay, honey, we can't change the past, you know that. All we can do is walk ahead one step at a time." He covered her hand with his and said, "I'm here, if you want to talk. Right now I think I'll give you some time. How about I go get us a couple of chairs? We'll sit by the ocean."

"Yes, Brent, that would be lovely, thank you. And, yes, I do need a little time."

Ashton watched Brent walk away and she had such a mix of emotions. She knew she loved Brent but it was nothing like the feeling she had experienced with Ryan, or that feeling of breathless surrender that she felt with Karl.

But, then, she and Ryan's lovemaking had always been hurried and slightly uncomfortable. Necking in dorms wasn't conducive to passionate lovemaking. Roommates, time constraints, all the embarrassment of something new. She and Ryan never even spent a whole night together.

She finished up breakfast and walked to the water's edge. She wandered up to the two chairs Brent ordered. He was swimming, gesturing for her to come in. She dropped her caftan on the chair and walked back to the water. Watching Brent, she thought, maybe it's time to be practical.

"Ashton, c'mon, race you to the buoy."

Side by side, they swam in tandem. Brent was just a bit ahead and determined to win. Ashton turned over — the salt water was a cradle of warmth and the sun was dazzling.

"Oh Brent, this feels so good."

"Told 'ya. Let's go be lazy."

They swam back to the shore and slipped under the welcoming shade of the beach umbrellas. Their comfort and ease were palpable. Brent handed Ashton a sparkling water and got one for himself.

"Ashton," Brent sat up in the lounge, "You know what I've told you is true. I love you and I want very much for us to spend the rest of our lives together. Let's stop this back and forth. It's quite simple. Come on Ashton, let's get married."

There was a long silence and Ashton looked into Brent's handsome face. "I need to think about this Brent. This is a really big step and I want to be calm and sure. Give me a couple of days and I promise I'll answer."

"OK, I accept the time frame. And then, we'll go pick out a ring you love, together. How about that?"

"Alright, Brent, do you have to fly back tomorrow?

"I scheduled a virtual meeting today, but I don't think I can postpone the final details of this merger. I should know more by tonight. It's actually done me some good to be away from my usual routine. So, let's enjoy this spectacular day."

Ashton mused, "Isn't it strange to feel so calm and so easy about a marriage proposal? Isn't that strange?" Ashton settled back into the lounge sipping her sparkling water. She put her sunglasses on and relaxed. This is all going to work out. I know it will and the calm and the comfort I feel right now — I may not even need two days. She turned to look at Brent. He was calm, too, and Ashton thought, "Wow, what a relief, no drama."

They enjoyed the beauty of the day and talked like the old friends they were. It was comfortable.

"Hey Ashton, what time should we meet for dinner?"

"Let's make it early tonight. How is 6:00 PM?"

"Great. See you then, Beautiful Lady. You inspired me, I've booked a massage for myself."

"Oh, Brent they're really good. You're going to feel like a million, see you later."

Ashton smiled, "I'm turning into a mermaid. All I do is swim and take showers. But my, this feels good: the sun, the salt water, and that beautiful air."

And she liked the thoughts that we're going through her head. "Ashton, Brent is someone who really loves you. Not wildly, but steadily and true."

She had a feeling she already knew her decision, but there was something she had to do first.

Chapter Thirty

The sun pouring in the window awakened Ashton and her phone was ringing.

"Ashton, I've run into a bit of a snag, and I have to get back to the States. I leave today. I was able to get an early afternoon flight. How about breakfast?"

"Brent, OK, I'll be down in a few minutes."

"OK, Ashton, give me a half hour because I've gotta pack up and check out."

Ashton took her time under the shower. She put on her favorite Jurlique facial oil and slipped into her cream cotton skirt. A touch of her pink coral lipstick, her gold hoops, and she was ready for breakfast.

She sat at the table that was under the shade of the canopy. The sun was already blazing and glorious. Brent came down looking very much the way she always saw him. A suit jacket on one arm and a portfolio with a yellow pad and a pen tucked under the other.

He was frowning. But the moment he saw Ashton, a huge smile lit up his face. "Hi Beautiful. I think Australia agrees with you. Maybe it's just the sunlight, but I think you're getting more beautiful every day."

Ashton laughed, "Well, when a heart gets cracked open, more light gets in, right?

"Isn't that Leonard Cohen?"

"Yes, it is. I'm starving this morning." Ashton dug into breakfast.

After writing a few more paragraphs, Brent put down his legal pad and looked into Ashton's eyes. "Listen,

Honey, I'm really sorry I have to leave right now. But a virtual meeting isn't going to solve what I need to handle. I want you to know I think you and I will make a great team. We have so much going for us. Most of all, we're really good friends."

"Brent, I know that. In many ways, I don't need any convincing because I know you're right for me. I just want to take some time and do some writing. You know, I always do that. And it will help me sort it all out."

"Absolutely, I know you've been through a lot, but I also know, Ashton, that you and I love each other."

"You're right Brent, we do and we're lucky. I just want to be sure about the kind of love I feel. We'll zoom in a couple of days and in any case, I think it's about time for me to get back to the states, too."

"OK, well I guess it's time to get myself to the airport. I'll hear from you then, yes?

"Yes, Brent that's for sure. Oh and Brent, good luck with the merger."

He grabbed his coat and headed out. "Brent, thank you for staying and thank you for being here with me."

"It was the right thing for me to do."

Ashton finished her iced coffee and walked slowly out to the cabana set up for her. What a comfort it had been to have Brent here, but there was still Karl.

She pulled her journal out of her woven straw bag and settled back into the cushions under the shade.

"OK, girlfriend," she said to herself, "it's time to get real."

Ashton started writing.

Do I love Brent? Of course, I do. He's someone I can count on. I've been there for him; he's been there for me and we're really good friends. That's super valuable in any relationship. He's steadfast, and does what he says he's going to do. He's honest. He treats his employees well.

"Ashton, what's the matter with you? He's got everything any woman would be thrilled to have."

I know his family and we have known each other since we were little. We had the most wonderful summer vacations at the lake and down the shore — of course I love Brent. And one of the most exciting things about Brent is that he's not exciting.

Ashton froze in mid-thought.

"One of the best things about him is that he's not exciting. Oh, that's horrible. Why would I think that? Well, I don't mean that he's not exciting — what I mean is you can count on him, he's stable and he's sort of predictable. Do I want 'sort of predictable?' Well, yes, there wouldn't be any drama, there wouldn't be fights, there wouldn't be — heck, we didn't even fight when we were kids."

"'And it's high time, young lady,' Ashton could just hear her father saying, that you settle down and get married.' And you know something, Dad, you're right. It is time. Ashton chuckled to herself and sprayed on a little more sunscreen."

She opened the bottle of sparkling water and squeezed in a lime from the ice bucket beside her that was filled with treats. "Gee, I like this place, it's not over the top, but it's so soothing to the soul."

As Ashton took a sip of the sparkling water she thought, "Now let me look at this from the other side. So what do I do about Karl Van Ness? Do I just pretend this didn't happen? Ashton, you know yourself better than that. No way. Can you just forget about the feelings you have for this man?"

"Yes," she said aloud, "I'm going to forget about him and go take the swim."

The soothing water felt heavenly and suddenly she felt a tickling at her ankle. She looked into the clear water and there was a tiny fish nibbling at her ankles. She and the brightly colored creature played tag for a while and she found herself laughing with delight.

As she swam back to the shore, she was suddenly calm, and all the agitation she felt about Karl was gone. "Let's face the facts. I loved Ryan with all my heart but I'm not that person anymore and he doesn't even exist anymore. Karl van Ness set out to get revenge and make me fall in love with him — and it worked."

"I fell head over heels in love, but who wouldn't? He did everything in his power to seduce me and it worked. Of course, it did. He's a powerful man who's used to getting his way. Karl has almost no relation to Ryan except for those gorgeous eyes. Who am I kidding?"

"Yes, he thought I deserted him. I get that my parents used their influence and their money and that they lied to me and that's wrong. I know. But they were trying to protect me. If I didn't love them so much, I'd hate them. I don't like it, and I'm going to have it out with my Dad when I get back, and tell them both what I think."

"But the fact is, love isn't about revenge. Love is love. Why didn't Karl talk to me? Why didn't he tell me the truth?"

"One thing I've got to do," Ashton decided, "I have to be straight with him and tell him that I've decided I know exactly what I'm doing."

And with that, Ashton gathered up her things and literally marched back to her room.

She put in a call to Evelyn, "It's Ashton."

"My dear, how are you? I was thinking about you this morning."

"Well, Evelyn, I have made a decision that I think is best for all concerned. It makes such logical sense. My heart can't take anymore drama and I just want peace and calm. I'm going to marry Brent. This makes sense."

Ashton heard an intake of breath. There was a pause and Evelyn said, "Ashton, have you really thought this out? Since when have you known love to be sensible?"

"But don't you realize that Karl set out to make me love him as revenge? It wasn't love, it was anger and fury. I mean, I don't blame him. I understand that he thought I deserted him. The fact is, I didn't. I just can't believe that he would lie to me like that."

"Ashton, I didn't give you details because I didn't want to influence you, but Karl has been desolate. He's running the hotel doing his job, but his heart is just not in it. He is walking through his days like a ghost. I haven't seen him this is sad and depressed since he knew you were gone ten years ago. He's become reclusive and almost impossible to deal with. He's thrown himself into work and there seems to be a perpetual scowl on his face. And when he's not scowling, his sadness shows to anyone with eyes to see."

"He hired a detective to find you, but then he admitted to me that he let him go." Evelyn was silent again and then she spoke very softly. "Ashton, I understand your reasoning and it does makes sense. But does it make heart sense? Is this what your heart wants? "

"Evelyn, I don't think it matters much what my heart wants anymore. I haven't had particularly good luck with this love stuff."

"Does that mean," Evelyn murmured, "that you don't love Brent?"

"Of course, I love Brent. He's like a part of my family, of course I love him. It makes logical sense. We know with each other there won't be any surprises and Brent is the most honest, supportive man I know."

"All right my dear, I'm not going to try to dissuade you from anything. You sound like you have your mind made up. One thing I'm going to ask you again is to please call Karl and meet with him one more time before you leave. Sit down and clear the air. Both of you need this. You know you do."

"You two have an intense history together, even though there was a space of years in between that history.

His love for you gave him the courage to live and then his anger at you not being there gave him the courage to walk into a new life. But do you realize that at the center of it all, it was always you, Ashton? Do you realize that?"

Ashton swallowed and found herself close to tears, "OK, Evelyn, I promise, yes, I'm going to call him now. Evelyn, thank you. You've been so kind. I never expected that."

Ashton hung up and suddenly she felt the tears spill down her cheeks.

Chapter Thirty-One

When Ashton dialed Karl's number, she discovered her hands were shaking. She got his answering machine. "Karl, it's Ashton, we need to talk. Please call me and let's arrange it as soon as possible. I need to make plans to get back to the States, but I want to talk with you before I leave. Please call me."

She ordered a Caesar salad and had just hung up when the phone rang. She saw it was Karl and almost didn't have the courage to pick up

"Ashton, where do you want to meet?"

"Karl, oh Karl," and without warning Ashton was crying.

"Ash, why are you crying? Are you OK? His voice was hard but there was a sound in the center of it that melted her heart."

"I've made some important decisions, Karl, and I think it's only fair that I share them with you. I want us to clear the air. We've meant too much to each other earlier in our lives and now . . . and . . . I know I have to talk to you. "Karl I'm at . . ."

"I know Ashton. I know exactly where you are."

"You know? Well then, why? How dare you check up on me?"

"I dare because . . . I always keep track of the people I love. And no matter what happens Ash, I have loved you."

Ashton sputtered, "Well, we'll talk about that."

Karl's voice was annoyingly calm. "Yes, my dear, we'll talk. And that's why I'm coming there so that we can talk. I can get there by 9 in the morning. All right. Ashton, I . . . I'll see you tomorrow. Sleep well." And with a click he was gone.

Ashton was tied up in knots. The sound of his voice turns the world upside down. All the anger she felt was gone. There was nothing but pain and a flood of tears. How on earth could she marry Brent when she felt this way about Karl?

Ashton looked at the clock for the hundredth time and it was 4:45 AM. Lord, what a night. I feel like I haven't slept a wink. Ashton climbed out of bed and went out on the balcony. There was a faint hint of dawn beginning to color the sky.

She ran back in and grabbed her journal and a pen. She wanted to write but it was still too dark and she didn't even know what to write. She was going to see Karl again. Karl, who wasn't Ryan anymore. The thought of seeing him made her body quiver. This was not going to be easy.

Ashton got up and leaned against the railing. She opened her arms to the sky and said out loud, "Angels, nature, all the gods that be, please give me the courage to speak from my heart today when I see Karl. Give me the courage to ask all the questions I need answered. Give me the courage to ask for what I want." She stopped and shook her head, "What do I want?"

The sky lit up with all the glorious colors of the dawn. Ashton began writing. She surprised herself when she discovered she was writing a letter to Karl.

Karl. Who are you? Are you the sensitive young man I was going to marry a decade ago? Have you loved many women? Are you filled with passion, or is it only anger?

Did you seduce me just for revenge? Did you feel anything for me, or was it all an act?

How could you believe I would desert you? I didn't know, Karl. I swear I didn't know you were still alive. The looks on my parents' faces, the looks they gave each other, shaking their heads, when I asked for you. What they did was wrong, they lied by omission, but they lied.

We both know they never approved of our relationship. That's why we were running away. We loved each other, and we were willing to take any risk to be together.

I know all you could go by were the facts. If I still loved you, I would have been there beside you. I understand that. My parents took advantage of my grief and rushed me to Villa Pierrefeu in Switzerland. That first year all I did was study and cry and was not really a participant, not even in my own life. I was dead inside. I had lost you and everything I imagined for our life together was gone. It never even entered my mind to ask questions. I accepted what they told me or didn't tell me. Oh Karl, please, please forgive me. And I hope somewhere in my heart, I can forgive myself.

In these past years I've dated a few people, and through it all, there was always Brent. He's a dear friend and someone who cares about me. I never let myself love anybody until I met you. I looked in your eyes and my heart almost stopped. I knew you, but you were a stranger.

And I fell, Karl, I fell in love with you. I've never felt anything like what you and I shared, not even with Ryan. Doesn't that sound ridiculous? But I don't know how else to express it. You're a completely different man.

I suspect there's too much pain between us for there ever to be a return to the love we've shared. It had — and has — so many dimensions. Oh, Karl, how I wish this had turned out differently.

But I hope you understand that for all these reasons, I've decided to marry Brent. It makes complete and logical sense. He's always been in my life and he's kind and he's loving. He is someone I like and admire. There's so much pain between us, Karl, that I don't think it could ever work.

Ashton saw drops of water on the page and realized that she was crying. She threw the journal down. "No, I'm not going to do this. I'm going to get calm. I'm going to take a shower. I'm going to put on war paint. I'm going to look like a million bucks and I am going to face Karl Van Ness calmly."

When Ashton came out of the shower, she was startled to discover her eyes were shining and her cheeks were flushed. She patted herself dry and sat at the dressing table, applied sunscreen, a sheer beigy gold with a shimmer on her eyelids and waterproof mascara. "Yes, I'm a practical woman — waterproof mascara. No matter what happens, I'm not going to have black streaks on my face." Then she applied her coral pink gloss on her lips and through all of this, although outwardly calm, her stomach was doing somersaults.

She slipped her gold hoops in her ears and put on her beautiful La Perla undies. The rosy beige blended into her skin and the delicate lace, a perfect complement. I need to feel at my best, strong, and confident.

"So, what shall I wear? Hmm . . . something sophisticated like my linen pantsuit?"

She tried on the pants, slipped on a cami under the jacket and thought, "No, that's not it," and threw them on the bed. Then she tried on one of her silk caftans, looked in the mirror and said, "No, it's too easy breezy, this is serious." She threw that on the bed, too. She tried on her cream cotton pants with the jeans jacket — she hated it. She threw it on the bed.

And there, there it was, a simple flowy dress that brushed her ankles. It perfectly matched the teal of her Amalfi sandals. She adjusted the off the shoulder neckline and added her favorite gold bangles. She put her hair up into a messy French twist with three tortoise shell hair pins, and then nestled a white orchid the hotel had placed on her dressing table into the curve of the French twist.

"There, I feel beautiful!" She looked in the mirror and almost didn't recognize this glowing, determined woman. "O, Angels, please give me the courage to say what I need to say." At that moment, the hotel phone rang.

"Ms. Ashton, Mr. Van Ness is here. He'll be downstairs near the pool." She almost dropped the phone. She sat down on the edge of the bed, shaking, and concentrated on breathing in and breathing out. It was about all she could manage at the moment.

Chapter Thirty-Two

Ashton pushed the button for the elevator but couldn't make herself stand still. She turned and headed down the stairs. When she got to the pool level, her heart was beating so hard that she couldn't breathe. She made herself walk deliberately, "Karl?" She seemed to be speaking to herself. The joy that rose at the sight of him shocked her. At that same instant, she heard her inner voice very clearly: "Remember this man has lied to you, you can't trust him."

Karl stood up and opened his arms. Ashton took three more quick steps and rushed into his arms. The instant she felt the electricity between them, she put her palm on his chest and straightened her back. She pulled away. Karl didn't want to let go, but the look in Ashton's eyes stopped him. He held out his hand and when Ashton took it, his touch felt like fire coursing through her veins. "Karl, thanks for coming so quickly."

He pulled out her chair, "You look wonderful, how are you?" His navy blue linen jacket made his eyes a darker blue.

Ashton looked out to the ocean and asked the waiter for a cappuccino with a shot of espresso.

"Ashton, would you like a little breakfast?" She nodded. Karl asked the waiter for croissants and some fresh fruit.

They were both so uneasy, they didn't know what to say. The silence between them seemed endless and suddenly both of them spoke at the same time.

"Ash."

"Karl." They both smiled.

"Ladies first."

"Both of us have gone through so much, and there's so much pain between us. It's so much, and so deep, that I don't think we can ever come to peace about it." Karl was about to answer and she raised her hand, "Karl, please let me finish. It's very important that I tell you this to your face."

"When I came here, Brent, my family friend, followed. He's asked me to marry him." Karl's eyes turned cold. "Please don't say anything yet, Karl, please let me finish. This isn't easy. I've known Brent since I was a little girl, and he's like part of my family. It makes sense and it will be very natural and easy for us to be together so . . . I'm going to marry Brent."

Karl's eyes darkened into glittering ice. The muscle in his jaw was pulsing.

His voice was strangled, "Ashton, you can't really think this is the best thing for you to do. Why? Because you think it's logical? Because you know him? You know me, too. You were going to marry me, for heaven's sake, or don't you remember that?"

"Of course, I remember that, Karl."

"You can't do this, Ash. You don't love him."

"How do you know I don't love him? Of course, I love him."

"What, like a brother? Have you made mad, passionate love with him, too?"

"Well, no. But sex and everything . . . changes after a few months of marriage anyway."

"Oh really, who told you that? It's not true Ashton. Please, don't throw your life away. Please." Karl took a deep shuddering breath, "Please forgive me, Ashton, give me a chance. Please, let's keep talking. I know we can work through this."

"Work through this? What's happened to the calculating Karl Van Ness ? Why are you all of a sudden being so touchy feely?"

"Damn it woman, I'm not being touchy feely. I love you. I have loved you from the moment you ran into me at the library. I looked at you and I felt something I'd never felt before. I know I buried that in a hole somewhere. But Ashton, I've never stopped loving you. The anger and the fury was there, but right next to it was the love, too. Can't you believe that? Don't you remember everything we felt? And what happened to us over the last week is so far beyond where we were when we were going to get married. Ashton, I love you. I have always loved you."

"Oh, even when you were being the Casanova of Australia and assorted other countries?"

"Yes, even when I was Casanova or Don Juan or whoever the hell you want to call me."

They were on their second coffee, and neither had touched a bite of breakfast.

"Ashton, let's go for a walk on the beach? Let's cool down and let's keep talking."

"All right. I guess we owe each other that."

Ashton gestured to Mark to put out a cabana for two. "I'll get right on that, Ms. Cameron."

They both reached for a croissant and Karl broke off a piece of his, buttered it, and offered it to Ashton. As she bit into the beautiful texture, she remembered the moment at Le Lys Blanc when Karl fed her the caviar. She shivered in spite of the warmth of the morning sun.

Karl rolled up his pants and Ashton took off her sandals in silence. They left them under the nautilus shell canopy, and began walking along the shore – the silence stretching between them.

Then Ashton said, so quietly he could barely hear, "Karl, I can't believe you thought I deserted you."

"You weren't there. "

Ashton said very softly, "Please, let me continue. I really need to say this to your face Karl. After the accident, I was very lucky. I was only in the hospital for a few days with cuts and scratches and I had a mild concussion. When I woke up in the hospital, my family was there. They were standing around and I remember the look on their faces.

When I spoke, they were all so amazed that I was OK. I ached everywhere, but apart from that, I was fine. Then my father took my hand and said, "Princess, we're awfully happy to have you back." I searched all the faces but you weren't there. My heart sank and their expressions told me what I feared. That you were dead. I tried to ask, but I couldn't stop crying. Brent was there holding my hand and I begged him to tell me the truth. I remember he shook his head, "No, Honey, he didn't make it."

"After I left the hospital, we never spoke about the accident again. My parents never mentioned if the police had given them my duffel bag, or if they knew I was eloping with you that night. We just never spoke about it again. "

"Ryan . . . I can't call you Ryan. There's nothing about you that's like Ryan except your eyes, and even your eyes don't look the same. Your expression is different. You're a different man."

"Karl, you know they didn't approve of our relationship and tried everything to send me on trips and to finishing school. They did that the whole time we were together. They thought that time away from you would change how I felt. I'd been fighting them every step of the way. Suddenly there was no longer a reason to fight. So, I went to Switzerland and the rest, well you know the rest."

"Ashton, I confess I couldn't believe that someone as intelligent as you wouldn't have investigated or checked. If I was dead, why wouldn't you stay for the funeral?"

"Oh Karl, I couldn't. Every time I thought of you, I remembered the horrible noise of our car skidding and of the impact, of you holding my hand. Somehow, I couldn't move beyond that moment. I'm so deeply sorry that I wasn't there for you. I promise you, had I known, I would have been there by your side, night and day."

"I was lucky, Evelyn was there, and she really is a guardian angel in my life. Her care and her kindness were astounding. She researched the best doctors in the business to rebuild my shattered body. When the doctors removed the bandages on my face, I literally didn't recognize myself. There was swelling, of course. My cheekbones were different because they had broken, my jaw was wired shut, my nose belonged on a Roman statue and the angle of my jaw was different. Everything was different."

"I spent years, Ashton, two years, in recovery. It took me almost six months to be able to walk. I had to learn how to do that again. The pain was excruciating. Through it all, Evelyn was there. She had her people fix me special meals and mopped my brow when the sweat dripped down my face as I struggled to walk between the parallel bars."

"Ashton, please forgive me. Forgive me for not believing that you didn't know. When I saw you enter the ballroom my fingers went numb."

"Oh, so that's why you dropped the glass? I saw that. And I wondered who you were."

"You took my breath away. You were more beautiful than I remembered you. And I admit, when I realized you didn't recognize me, a tsunami of rage and anger washed over me. And right then I knew, I knew I was going to make you love me and then I was going to drop you flat just the way you left me. Oh, Ashton, how could I be so stupid?"

"Karl, if I put myself in your shoes even for a moment, I realize I might have done the same thing. I know that doesn't make it hurt any less."

"Do you suppose, Beauty, that maybe we've gone through so much that for the rest of our lives we never have to face that kind of pain again?"

"Karl, that's a beautiful thought."

They kept walking, their shoulders almost touching.

Chapter Thirty-Three

Ashton looked at Karl and her heart beat faster. His profile was. . . what a handsome man he was. The surgeon's hand, and the years, had turned a nice looking young man into a devastatingly handsome one. The sharpness of his jaw was such a great contrast to the gentleness of his mouth.

They sat down on a teak bench under a frangipani tree.

"Ashton, I know you feel you're being practical and logical. I understand that darling. I've done it for years. I was so proud of myself thinking that I had managed to separate my love for you. I put it away in a part of me I couldn't reach, but every time you looked at me as we grew closer, the love that I had put away so carefully was coloring my every action."

"When I brought you the three envelopes you were like a little girl overcome with delight. Ashton, that thrilled me because it brought you joy. Darling, please, please whatever you do, don't marry a man who doesn't make your heart beat faster. Don't marry a man who doesn't make you convulse with laughter and whose touch thrills you now, and my darling Ashton, will still thrill you, years from now."

Karl moved closer to her on the bench and wrapped his arm around her shoulders. He tilted her face up to his, "Darling, my darling Ashton, I loved you as Ryan, and after all I've experienced in this world, I love you even more as Karl. You're a precious being in my life and because I found you again. I can't imagine living without you. I love you, Ashton Cameron."

Karl's eyes were bright with unshed tears. "Karl, Karl, I want to trust you. We've been apart for over a decade and had such different experiences. But Karl, I love you, too."

Their eyes locked and everything else fell away. The spicy rose fragrance of the frangipani tree surrounded them. Ashton breathed in his scent, Vetiver, and the love in his eyes was turning to passion.

Ashton got up and turned to him, "Karl, let's go for a swim. Are you here for the day?"

"I'm here for as long as it takes. I already checked in."

They walked together closer to the shore now, their shoulders touched, their hands instinctively reached for each other and their fingers intertwined. It felt so right. It was comfort and passion combined.

Ashton pulled her hand away and faced Karl. "OK, let's go back to the hotel, and I'll beat you to our cabana, and see you in 30 minutes precisely."

She was laughing and Karl said, "You really think you can beat me?

"Of course I can, I am a gazelle!"

"And I'm a lion, and I'm gonna get you!" He roared at her, and they were running across the sand, laughing.

Karl sprinted ahead, turned back and watched Ashton running toward him, her hair flying in the wind. "Oh gazelle of mine, you've lost your hair pins."

"Oh, Karl, I love those."

They retraced their steps and Karl found two of them, Ashton found the other one.

Karl said, "I believe you dropped your orchid too, oh lovely gazelle."

Both breathless from running, Karl placed her hairpins in her outstretched hand. He seized her other hand, looked in her eyes, "I'm not going kiss you until you beg me to kiss you."

"Well, you can wait until pigs fly then, because I'm not going to ask you."

"We'll see about that," his head thrown back, Karl laughed.

When Ashton got up to her room she was so filled with exhilaration and fun, delight, and confusion that she didn't know what to do.

"Well, of course I know what to do, I'll put on my gorgeous new bikini, and I am going to make Karl Van Ness kiss me — not the other way around." But somehow, all she could do was laugh. What a way to go to war, laughing!

She put her hair back in a ponytail, adjusted her gold belly chain, slipped into her Amalfi sandals, and put on her sexy new teal bikini. She grabbed her beach bag and fairly flew down the stairs to the beach.

Karl was already there and had ordered mango juice and some sweet and savory appetizers to nibble.

"Well, since loving you had caused me to lose my appetite at breakfast, I thought we might need a little food."

"Oh, Karl, it's perfect." Ashton grabbed some carrots, and a couple of bites of delicious Spanish aged manchego cheese and asked, "Oh, Lion, do you want to kiss me yet?"

"Absolutely not, Miss Cameron. This is a contest I'm going to win."

"That's what you think." Ashton took off her kaftan and the look on Karl's face made her laugh out loud.

She sprinted for the water and jumped in. Karl was right behind her. "You have an unfair advantage."

"Why surely, kind Sir," Ashton teased with an exaggerated southern drawl, "I have no idea what you're talking about."

They played like two children splashing each other. Ashton swam up to Karl and put her arms around his neck. Her breasts were like two points of fire against his chest pushing through her bathing suit.

She brought her mouth close to his and said, "Hmm, so you want me to ask you to kiss me? I don't think I'm really in the mood." She was laughing so hard it was difficult to get the words out. "Oooo, and there seems to be a really big stick in the water? Gosh, that could be dangerous."

"You little minx. Do you want me to kiss you?"

"Certainly not! I'm allergic to you!" And Ashton swam away from him with strong strokes.

"Hey, I didn't know gazelles could swim. It's not fair."

"It's certainly fair, Mr. Tiger, leopard, lion, or whatever you are."

Karl swam after her, "Hey Ashton, I found something for you. "

"You can't trick me; I'm not getting close to you again."

"Yes, you will, how would you like a rare seashell? "How about a golden cowrie?" Karl held up an amazing shell. It's beautiful golden orange shone in the sun.

Ashton swam back to his side. "Oh Karl, that's gorgeous! But wait a minute, you don't find golden cowrie shells this close to shore. They are only found at great depths and this one. . . ." She turned the shell over. It still had its brown cover. "Is this alive?"

"No. Why don't we go back to the beach and explore this treasure?"

Seated on the chaise, Ashton removed the shell's cover to find cotton inside. She removed that, and there inside this perfect golden cowrie, was her engagement ring. The ring she left on the carpet when she left Karl a few days before. It was the ring she lost ten years ago when the accident tore their lives apart.

Karl was profoundly serious, "Ashton, let's take this second chance. Let's give each other the opportunity to share the magic we feel. We'll talk, we'll spend time, and we'll enjoy each other's company until your heart can peacefully decide what you want. In the meantime, while you're deciding, I need to return to you what is rightfully yours. Not only this ring, my beautiful partner, but also my heart. Ashton, will you marry me?"

Ashton found she couldn't speak and just nodded her head.

"Yes, you'll marry me? Or yes to the ring and my heart?"

"Yes, to the ring, and yes to your heart." Ashton held out her left hand and it was shaking. Karl slipped the ring on her finger. "I remember when you gave me this Karl, and yes, this is definitely mine. I don't know about marrying you."

"Well, how about an easier question, do you know whether you're going to have dinner or not this evening? Even gazelles must eat. How about coming to my lair at 6:00 tonight?"

"Sounds dangerous, and quite irresistible. I'll see you then."

Ashton picked up her things and accepted the gorgeous shell from Karl's outstretched hands. She didn't say another word but squared her shoulders and walked away.

Chapter Thirty-Four

Ashton took a long bath with some of the essential oils she loved. She patted herself dry and Karl was all she could think about. "I love this man, and I can't command my own heart. I used to be able to, not anymore."

She looked down at the tiny diamond on her hand, when Karl gave her the ring a decade ago, he tied it on a bookmark and placed it inside a book she loved, *Cyrano de Bergerac*. He gave it to her while they were sitting in the little booth in a diner they both loved. It brought tears to her eyes then, and a decade later, it still did.

Ashton put on her bias cut cream silk with slender straps. The dress was almost backless, just thin straps holding the delicate fabric together. Just thinking of Karl and his reaction, she felt her nipples press against the silk. Yes, she was going to drive him quite mad, but then, she was already driving herself quite mad.

She slipped on her gold sandal heels and a jeweled bolero jacket. "And no matter what," she laughed, "I will not ask him to kiss me." She was laughing like a child and that's exactly how she felt. It was joyous and warm and the anticipation of seeing this gorgeous man again who stirred her heart and soul. . . . Who am I kidding? Yes, I want to marry this man.

She knocked on the door of his suite at precisely 6:00 PM. The door swung open to a beautiful room overlooking the ocean. There was a familiar fragrance and Ashton noticed a small vase with flowers from the frangipani tree.

Karl opened the Verve Clicquot Rosé champagne they had enjoyed at Le Lys Blanc. "I'm sorry, I don't have Monsieur Marchand's sword to open the champagne." Karl presented her with a crystal flute of the shimmering liquid. "Here's to the most beautiful woman in the world," he toasted her solemnly, and their glasses rang.

"I found something for you, Ashton, that I think you'll like." He handed her a small flat package tied with a gold ribbon. "I believe you were searching for this the first time we met."

Ashton sat down on the couch and untied the ribbons to discover an exquisite Italian leather box. When she opened that, she was greeted with one of her favorite books. But this one was very special. It was a first edition of *Cyrano de Bergerac*, 1898.

Karl sat down beside her and quoted softly:

No part of any day is forgotten if you were there:
I know that on the tenth of May last year
You had altered a little the way you wore your hair!
To me your hair is the heart of light.
And often, as it is when we have stared too long at the sun
Everywhere we look is flecked with red,
I turn away from watching you, and tread
A landscape dancing with your fire.

"Oh Karl, how beautiful, how thoughtful, and how perfect." They moved together to the balcony looking out at the waves lapping at the sand. A light breeze had sprung up, blowing in warm fresh air from the ocean.

The sunset was amazing, the sky ablaze. The evening was still warm, bathing the landscape with radiant, fiery hues and streaking the water with colors of purple and orange.

Karl put his arm around Ashton's waist and pulled her to him. "Well, my beauty, you're in the lion's lair, do you have any requests of me?"

Ashton smiled and looked up into those gorgeous eyes boring into hers. She wanted to continue playing and teasing, but her heart was clamoring for attention. "Yes, I do have a request for you . . . ahhhh, let's see . . . May I have some more champagne?"

"OK, beautiful woman, touché. Here is your champagne. Do you have any further requests for me?"

"Yes, Karl, I do. You've given me this ring and your heart and in exchange, I give you, my heart. Will you treat it kindly?"

Ashton's voice was so soft, Karl had to lean closer to hear her words. "And I have another request, Mr. Van Ness."

"Yes?"

Ashton's pulse was pounding, "Will you kiss me?"

His answer was to lift her up with a growl and carry her into the bedroom. Karl was kissing her ears, her neck, her hands, and Ashton was breathless with passion. She dropped the bolero she was wearing, and her nipples strained against the delicate silk fabric of her dress. Karl tore off his linen jacket and Ashton was unbuttoning his shirt, kissing his chest every time she unfastened another button. Karl pulled back the covers and laid her in the middle of the bed.

"So you want to be kissed, do you? *What are all these kissings worth if thou kiss not me?*"

Ashton's whole body was quivering with desire and love. "Does my Beauty want me as much as I want her? "

"Oh Karl, yes, I do. I want you, and only you."

He plunged into her wetness, and she wrapped herself around him and moaned with each thrust. They melded into one together and Ashton had never felt such tender, fierce, loving coupled with a peacefulness she had never known.

Karl rolled onto his back, moving Aston on top of him. Her hair fell around his face.

"My darling Ashton, do you know how much I love you? I don't want to live without you. Ashton, I want to enjoy life with you for the rest of my days, will you marry me?"

Ashton gazed down at him — that handsome face so filled with hope, love, fear of rejection, and sadness. That beloved face.

"Karl, I've stopped wrestling with my heart. I love you. I love you no matter what your name is. And you're right, it's a miracle we found each other again. I don't want to spend the rest of my life without you, either. Yes, Karl Van Ness, I will marry you."

She looked into the eyes of the man she loved, the beautiful, deep blue eyes of the ocean. Those eyes filled with love, smiled back at her. Ashton, whose heart had been ready to break with sorrow the day before, was filled with joy.

"Ashton, I loved you before, I love you now. You have always been, and always will be, the only woman in my heart, and in my life."

The End